A Small Town is a World

Born in 1919, David Kossoff has become widely known for his acting in films and on stage and for his television performances, retelling stories from the Bible. His one-man stage shows have also added to his very large following.

D1350967

Also by
David Kossoff in Pan Books

You have a minute, Lord?

A Small Town is a World

The 'Rabbi Stories' of

David Kossoff

Illustrated by the Author

Pan Books London and Sydney

First published 1979 by Robson Books Ltd
This edition published 1980 by Pan Books Ltd,
Cavaye Place, London SW10 9PG
© David Kossoff 1979
ISBN 0 330 26226 2
Reproduced, printed and bound in Great Britain by
Cox & Wyman Ltd, Reading

Author's Note

Somebody once said that there are only seven basic 'jokes'. Perhaps that somebody meant that the basic human situations from which spring all stories, funny or sad, are few. Right; no argument. Also true is that wine, in the main, is made from grapes. And that cheese comes from milk. No argument. But every country has its own wine and its own cheese, of a special flavour belonging only to that country. Certainly it is true that some legends and folk humour tales are common to a number of countries. So are grapes and milk. It's the local flavour that is different. It's the endless permutations that have amused us and attracted the collectors of such humour for a long time. We owe the collectors a lot. This book is a sort of thank-you to them. They deserve more honour than they receive, for they are no less single-minded and industrious than the 'creative' or 'original' writers, many of whom owe much to their less exalted colleagues.

The collectors are the detectives. They follow trails. They go everywhere. In Jewish lore they move confidently from the Talmud to Brooklyn, from King David to King Arthur, from the seventy-two scribes of Eleazar to Finklestone of the *Jewish Daily News*.

Honour then, friends, the names of Cahan and Shindler and Gaster and Finzberg and Friedlander and Vilnay and Hurwitz. Collectors all, who used rare taste in selection and great skill in translation. Finally, and personally, my thanks to the great Nathan Ansubel, collector of collectors, whose *Jewish Folklore* and *Jewish Humour* have been a joy in our home for thirty years.

D.K.

Preface

There is no such place as the Klaneshtetl of this book. Once there were a hundred places like Klaneshtetl. The *klaneshtetls*, the little towns, of that Western part of Russia that took in Poland and Lithuania and which was known in the eighty years before the Revolution as the Pale of Settlement. A vast area where at the turn of the century five million Jews lived, with no choice. The Pale was created by Imperial decree to put Jews in. It was ruled harshly and life was hard. But the life was *Jewish*, and a great flowering of activity took place at every cultural level. In literature, in political thought, in education, in religion and matters of the spirit.

There was widespread poverty. Yet from the poverty and hardship of those times came some of the richest humour we know. From that world came the marvellously-observed tales of Sholom Aleichem and Peretz and Mendele Mocher Sforim. Of Asch and Babel and Der Tunkeler.

Yiddish was the language. That polyglot tongue as rich in fine nuance and delicate shades of meaning as English, which has about five times as many words. Mind you, it owes as much to its use and inflection as to its vocabulary. The hands play a part too, the shoulders, the eyebrows, the pauses, the words left *un*said. As a language it is considered untranslatable, and it may be so, despite the multi-language versions of the great writers just named.

Yet for a very long time Yiddish was the one truly universal tongue. The language of the Diaspora, the dispersed-all-over-the-world Jews. A wandering, moved-on people. It was practical to have a language that travelled well. The penniless immigrant in a new and frightening country would soon be given succour by people as poor as himself, from other parts of the world, who would share what they had, including the most immediate comfort, the same language.

This book is not a translation. I heard Yiddish as a child, but neither speak nor understand it well. It is a dying language, which is at once both good and bad. Bad because the loss of any of the roots of a people is bad. And good because the need for it is less. The immigrants of yester-year are the established families of today, speaking only the language of the country they finished up in. Now their children learn a 'new' Jewish language, far far older than Yiddish. Hebrew. Once the language only of the prayer book and now again the language of a nation, Israel, where

10

the Dispersion began. Full circle. Lately, it is said, the practical and tough Israeli shows increasing interest in the language of his grandparents. When a thirty-year-old country displays such interest it does not mean a weak nostalgia or a lack-of-confidence immaturity. It means the opposite. A coming of age.

1

The Rabbi found himself on this Friday morning a little bit tired of hearing about other people's troubles. In a small town like Klaneshtetl, everyone knew everybody else's business and there were no secrets. But Rabbi Mark was there and they trusted him and they paid his wages and they used him endlessly. And it was the end of a hard winter and things had not been easy and everybody went with their troubles to the Rabbi, who had a few little troubles too, and who could *he* go to? Only to his wife Sophie, and he wouldn't do that. Not just now. She hadn't been well, and *that* had been a trouble too. Still, thank God, she was on the mend and he would manage. He had broad shoulders for trouble, the Rabbi, and humour also, and as many times in the past, he looked at the problem of his flock's troubles with a glint of humour. A plan emerged, and at the evening service he said he would, next day, on the Sabbath, make an important announcement, in the synagogue.

The place was crowded. Mark looked around, his sensible middle-aged eyes missing nothing. 'My sermon today,' he said, 'spoke of God's help with heavy loads. Well, it seems to me that in this town everybody has heavy loads and everybody could do with some help. Many of you have come to me and told me of your sack of trouble, your "peckel" of trouble. Many of you have said to me, "Rabbi, nobody has a peckel like mine. *No*body." It worries me that I can't do much to help.

'So,' said the Rabbi, 'I asked God, and in a dream I was shown a way, if not to help, at least to give you a rest from your peckels. Everybody says that their peckel is the heaviest and that nobody else can have trouble like they've got. Am I right?'

'It's true,' murmured the congregation. 'It's true. How can anyone else know the troubles we've got? Sacks. Peckels.'

The Rabbi waited for silence. 'In the next week,' he said, 'everybody will write his troubles on pieces of rock and put the rocks in a sack, a peckel. On Friday you will bring the peckels to my house and leave them outside my door, and for the whole weekend I will look after them. You will be absolutely free of your troubles for a whole weekend.'

There was an excited hubbub as people saw the great wisdom of their Rabbi. 'And,' said their Rabbi loudly and clearly, 'and, on Monday morning you can all come and take away any peckel you like! Is it agreed?'

The congregation roared their approval of this marvellous plan, and it was done, and by tea-time the next Friday the pile of sacks of rocks outside the Rabbi's door was huge and the town (and the Rabbi) had a peaceful and happy weekend, with smiling faces and splendid singing at the services.

On Monday morning the Rabbi got up early and watched from his window. The townspeople gathered in front of the pile of peckels and looked and weighed up and considered. Then each took away his own, and the Rabbi went and had his breakfast.

2

The Rabbi and Sophie were giving supper to a favourite guest. Isaac the Beggar, who not only was good company, with wonderful stories of his wandering life, but who also had recently brought off a coup that had made the whole town laugh. It had begun at this very table, in Mark's house, a few weeks before. The supper talk had been of the little hospital in the town, which was always short of money. For a new stove, logs for burning, blankets, repairs, everything. There was no State aid; it was the town's business.

Isaac had pondered. 'Long ago, Rabbi,' he said, 'about the time you first came here to Klaneshtetl, we had a doctor called Molka. He was born here and the town helped him to go away to University to become a doctor. He gave us a year or two and then went to Moscow where he is now a great man called Professor Molkonin.'

'I remember him,' said Sophie, who'd been

16

born in the town. 'Perhaps he would help the hospital. He worked there, he comes from Klaneshtetl, and he's Jewish.'

'Not according to him,' said Isaac. 'Moscow born and bred and positively not Jewish. He is the head of a large teaching hospital. A famous lecturer and surgeon. His lecture theatre named after him. Very rich indeed. Friend of the Czar, who he treats for dandruff. I think I'll go and see him.'

'The Czar?' said Mark, chuckling.

'Molkonin – Molka,' said Isaac.

'For dandruff?' said Mark.

'For money,' said Isaac. And was gone next day. Mark did not give it too much thought. The Beggar often went off to far-off places. Famous. A leader of his profession.

Oddly, Mark heard the story first, not from Isaac, but in a letter from a friend in Moscow who worked at the Molkonin hospital.

The Beggar had presented himself, with fur cap, boots and bundle, in the Great Man's waiting room. Who sent you? he was asked. Nobody. Appointment? No. Money? No. Quite impossible then. Then I'll wait.

He waited six days, in fur cap and muddy boots. From the bundle, strong-smelling cheese and garlic sausage. Black village bread.

The Professor, they at last told him, uses in his lectures poor patients who are ill. You can join them. Tomorrow morning. Without clothes. Can I keep on the cap, and the boots? Very well.

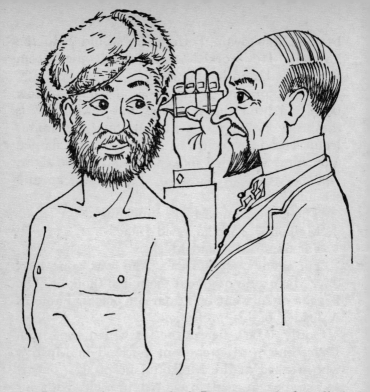

Lecture theatre packed. Isaac at end of the line. Enter Molkonin, obviously held in great respect. Each patient shown, discussed and dismissed. Now it's Isaac's turn. In fur cap, boots and nothing else. Wiry, muscular, weather-beaten. Steady eyes.

'A new patient,' said the Professor. 'Not seen before. How can I help you, my friend?'

'You can help us both, my friend,' said Isaac. 'You can give me a large donation for the Klaneshtetl Hospital.'

18

The Beggar helped himself to another piece of Sophie's plum-cake. 'Not a bad fellow really,' he said. 'Examined me carefully, looked into my ears – at the same time telling me to keep my mouth shut – declared me healthy, put me up overnight and gave me my fare home and 10,000 roubles.'

'For keeping your mouth shut?' said Mark.

'For Klaneshtetl Hospital,' said Isaac.

3

It was the end of the afternoon and the Rabbi had not had a good day. The day had started badly and rather earlier than usual. In the middle of the night in fact. He'd got in very late from a house of mourning in the next village and he'd quietly and gently got into bed beside Sophie, deep in the sleep of a dutiful wife. The Rabbi had relaxed with a great tired sigh. A silence. Then Sophie said: 'Close the window, Mark, it's cold outside.'

The Rabbi stayed quiet.

'Mark,' she said, 'close the window. It's cold outside.'

Mark snuggled deeper.

'Mark,' she said.

'I heard, I heard,' said the Rabbi. 'You want me to close the window.'

'Well, it's cold outside.'

'And if I close the window,' said the Rabbi, 'it'll be warm outside?'

So the Rabbi's bad day had really begun the night before. Getting out of bed he'd trodden on his own shoe and turned his ankle and stumbled and bruised his elbow on the wardrobe corner. Then he knocked over the little table with the glass of water on.

'Why,' asked the nearly-asleep-again Sophie, 'are you making so much noise closing the window?' And the day had gone on like that. Hardly anybody at the morning service other than the ten old men without whom there could be no service, and they were quarrelsome and tetchy and he'd had to listen to their disputes and complaints. And there were other things. Paperwork, which he hated, and petty troubles brought to him by people well able to settle such things themselves. Other people wanting him to take sides, or give approval to things that he could see no merit in at all. And it seemed that of all the sick people he had visited not one had been ennobled by their suffering. Not one. Well, perhaps one: Daniel, who'd been patient and smiling. But Daniel was only six.

The Rabbi, as always, hoped for something or somebody to brighten his day. It didn't always happen. You had to hope and wait. As he was locking up his little office over the synagogue he heard from downstairs the voice of the grocer, Herman. 'Just going home, Rabbi?' said Herman.

'Yes, was there something you wanted?'

'Nothing important. It can wait. I'll walk with you to the market-place.'

The Rabbi liked Herman, who was blunt and sometimes funny without meaning to be. They chatted. 'Do you,' asked the Rabbi, 'know a man named Chiam Greenburg?'

Herman stopped, 'Chiam Greenburg? Chiam? Do I know Chiam Gr—? Mind you, I'm surprised *you* know him, Rabbi. I wouldn't have thought that he and you – although to just *know* him is all right. Not to do business with him; not to have dealings; to sign agreements; not to lend money to. Not to ask him a favour; to do anything for you; to keep his word.'

The Rabbi looked at Herman with great affection. Saviour of the day.

'Greenburg!' said Herman. 'Do I know – but *every*thing I know! Who he owes money to; his brother-in-law who won't talk to him; his wife who's carried a black eye more than once; his partner who doesn't trust him an inch!'

'You know him well,' said the Rabbi.

'And why shouldn't I?' said Herman. 'He's one of my closest friends. Goodbye, Rabbi.'

The Rabbi walked on, happily, a sermon forming in his mind.

4

It was quiet in the synagogue and the Rabbi was sitting with the old men and enjoying their endless discussion on fine points in the Holy Books.

He did not often have time to just sit, like other Rabbis in more important places. Here in the little town of Klaneshtetl he had many duties and little leisure. He did not lead in the discussion; the old men had their own ways and in any case regarded him as too young, despite his twenty-five years as Rabbi. He did not mind. He also learnt more than he could have taught. Not from the content of their talk as much as from their attitudes, which gave him a private joy, for a man of humour was the Rabbi.

Old Fogel was speaking. Telling a story. One of the miracle stories of which he seemed to have dozens. This one however was new to the Rabbi – and to the other greybeards who sat in rapt attention – except for Nathan the Pawnbroker

23

who was prone to scepticism and to argue about anything.

'. . . and there in the bushes was a baby,' old Fogel was saying. 'The old hermit who lived in the forest heard it and picked it up and took it home. It had been abandoned by a mother too poor to keep it. The old hermit had no money either, and no cow or goat for milk. He prayed to God, who heard and turned him into a woman and he was able to suckle the baby until it was weaned and then the hermit became a man again and the child and the hermit lived happily ever after. A wonderful story, yes? God is good.'

The other elders nodded, happy as children at the greatness of God. Not so the pawnbroker. The Rabbi spoke.

'Not happy, Nathan? Give us a word or two on it.'

'One must not abandon logic, even for such lovely stories, as Fogel should admit,' said Nathan. 'If God made the world and all living things including both a man and a woman it seems hard to believe that he would upset nature, the laws of which he made himself. It seems to me that it would have been just as easy for him to arrange for the hermit to find a bag of a thousand roubles and then engage a wet-nurse for the baby.'

The old men blinked, but there was no blasphemy here, no sacrilege. Who could know the ways of the Almighty? The Rabbi, observing the somewhat crestfallen Fogel who was fond of his miracles, and the rather triumphant Nathan who was smirking a bit, decided to stir the matter a little.

'Certainly,' he said to the pawnbroker, 'logic has its place. In the synagogue as in the home. In the study of the Talmud as in the running of a business or shop. Whether selling goods or,' he added, with mischief, 'holding goods against loans.'

Nathan took the bait. 'On the other hand,' he said, 'God is no fool. If he can change a man into a woman with so little trouble why should he advance a thousand roubles to a hermit, without security, free of interest, and with no hope of repayment. No, the story must be true.'

The discussion began and the Rabbi quietly left. Who could know the ways of the Almighty?

5

The Rabbi was happy. It had been a marvellous day. Who would have thought that in this little town of Klaneshtetl such a thing could have happened? Often his good wife Sophie was prone to say his sense of humour got him into scrapes, but this had been a joyous day – with an old friend to supper to recall old times at theological college and the rare and splendid hoaxes of those days. Now, full of Sophie's good food and the fine wine his guest had contributed to the meal, the two friends chuckled again. A marvellous day.

The Rabbi had known that Leon was coming for some time. They had not met for many years. Both had become rabbis but at different levels, as it were. Mark, from a small town, had settled in a small town. Leon, from the city, had taken up a post in a wealthy city community, married into a rich family who respected his calling, and had become a writer, teacher, and a famous lecturer upon the Talmud and the ancient Laws. A much-travelled popular speaker.

'Come to Klaneshtetl,' Mark had written to him. 'Here in our little synagogue we have some Elders who love to split hairs in argument and you would have a grand time with them. Stay with us. It's been so long. We can remember the old practical jokes together. Please come.'

Leon had agreed right away to make a loop in his next tour and come to Klaneshtetl. 'Mention of the jokes has given me an idea,' he wrote. 'More in my next letter, about Shmuel my coach driver.'

And the plan evolved. Shmuel, a loyal servant of Leon the great teacher, envied his master very much indeed. The respect and honour always shown him; the deference to his opinion; the hushed attention to his words. Poor Shmuel, who could hardly write his own name.

'How would you like, my old friend,' said Leon to Shmuel, 'to change clothes with me when we get to Klaneshtetl? I will drive and you will be the Rabbi-Teacher. We look roughly alike and my face is unknown there. You will have the speeches of welcome, the cakes and wine, and then we will go into the vestry and change clothes, and I'll do the Talmud discussion in the synagogue.'

And so it was. But the welcome and the wine both went to poor Shmuel's head and he would not change back into his clothes and marched, very majestic, into the synagogue, his 'driver' Leon enjoying every minute. Mark blinked, but

then, as host Rabbi, introduced the Talmud
passage for exposition by the learned visiting
teacher. A very difficult section indeed, and the
old men waited. Shmuel peered at the book
held open for him by one of the Elders. He could
not understand one word. Silence.

Then Shmuel spoke. 'You call this difficult to
understand? What's difficult? Even my own

driver could explain what is meant here. Where is he? Ah, there you are, driver. Come, tell these good people what it all means!'

'A marvellous day,' said Mark. 'Tomorrow, old friend, we will look for the moral in this matter. Raise your glass! To Shmuel.'

'To Shmuel,' said Leon.

6

The Rabbi was thoughtful. It was the time of the day that he found most conducive to having a quiet think. In his own small house, after his evening meal, with his feet up, and Sophie making quiet wifely noises in her kitchen.

He had pondered before on this matter, had Mark. This of the cursory attendance at synagogue by many of the townsfolk – except on the High Holy Days, or when there was trouble. The kind of trouble brought by bad weather, as of late, for the little town was in a largely agricultural province and a drought or too much rain or too long a winter could affect the lives of many.

Mark had posted up a notice that there would be a Service of Supplication. Of special prayer to the Almighty for help. He had done it a number of times before and had not been too happy at the half-grudging appearance by some, who came, took no real part in the Service, and left, having not said a word on their own or anybody else's behalf.

Mark had always found it easy to pray, to have a word with God, in his own words, relaxed and trusting. He tried to teach the children the same at the classes held in the little synagogue hall, but with not much success. There was much stilted thought in the town, and much superstition.

Sophie came in and sat down in her chair across the hearth from him. She respected the thinking going on, and was quiet. After a bit she said, 'A nice thing I heard today. Rivke's donkey had a colt. Mother and child doing well. An answer to prayer. A female colt.'

Mark smiled. Sophie had done this before. Dropped in a word or two to start a thought, to spark an idea when most needed.

'She prayed for a *female* colt? Not any colt? A female. Did she specify colour?'

'Yes. A white face and socks like the mother and if possible the brown of the father, which is what arrived. As asked for. Rivke is so happy.'

'So am I,' said Mark. 'For her, because she's got her baby donkey, and for me because I've got you.'

On the day of the special Service the little synagogue was full. It was cold too, for the winter was savage, endless. The people were wrapped up, cocooned in every kind of apparel. Faces could hardly be seen. Mark noticed again how many people just stood, hardly responding, leaving it all to him. He knew from bitter experience that those same people would say hurtful things if matters did not improve, if help did not come quickly.

'Your prayers maybe didn't get there, Rabbi,' they'd say. 'Maybe you chose the wrong words. After all you are no farmer. You don't know about orchards, about cattle, or sheep, or corn, or potatoes. Maybe the Almighty listens more carefully to an expert.'

All these remarks usually came from people who never said one word to the Almighty at any time.

It was time now for Mark's 'few words', for 'sermon' was the wrong name to call that bit of a special Service, he always thought. The people sat huddled close, those nearest the stove with steam rising from them.

Mark kept his tone cheerful, his voice encouraging and warm. He mentioned Rivke's new addition to the family.

'She prayed,' he said. 'She told God clearly what was in her heart, what she wished would happen. As I've told you before, I cannot prove to you that *every* prayer is heard. So it follows that if your prayer *does* come up, it would seem a good idea not to be vague. After all, you know best what you want. Why leave it to others?' Mark paused, and went on.

The huddled-together crowd showed no great interest in his words. They sat dully. It was true.

The Rabbi *had* said it before. What was *new*? And it was so *cold*. Who could say what was best to do? A Service, prayers, a few words from the Rabbi. Even if – what was that the Rabbi was saying? A *Roman*? What Roman?

'... and the Roman officer had great power, as all Romans did at that time,' Mark said, watching the heads come up and the faces appear. 'Worse than the Czar's soldiers, as cruel as the Cossacks. Pogroms were known before the fall of the Temple, you know.

'So here is the Roman on his way to Jerusalem to join his regiment. He has a problem. That morning his pack-donkey had given birth to a daughter, who was very unsteady indeed on her four thin little legs.

'From the other direction comes a poor man, all his worldly goods in a heavy sack on his back. That morning he had prayed. "Almighty," he'd said, "the sack is heavy and my feet are sore and swollen. A donkey, dear God, a donkey. A little donkey."

'Round the corner comes the Roman.

' "Here, you!" he orders. "Put your sack with my stuff on the pack-donkey."

' "A thousand thanks, your Honour," says the poor man, astonished.

' "– and pick up the little donkey and follow me, at the double," said the Roman.

'The poor man did as he was told. As he settled the little donkey across his shoulder he looked up.

33

' "Almighty," he said. "It's my own fault. I should have made clear that I meant that the donkey should carry *me*, not the other way round." '

Mark waited. Then a heavily-built man stood up. 'D'you mean, Rabbi, that if I was to tell God about the barn roof . . .?'

'Tell him about everything,' said Mark. 'What have you to lose?'

'Would he know about chickens?' said a woman.

'Ask him,' said Mark, 'in your own words. At any time.' He felt a bit happier. It looked as though some praying was to start.

7

The Rabbi had had a wearisome day and he was pleased it was over. As he opened the door of his little house Sophie came from the kitchen. 'You look a bit down, my love,' she said. 'We have a guest for supper who will cheer you up. Berel the Cantor.'

Mark was pleased. Indeed an old friend. Old Berel, who for more years than people could remember had travelled the country with his vast knowledge of liturgical music, ready to step in at a moment's notice to provide all the sung parts of any service of the year. He was a sort of treat, for many synagogues were too poor, too small to afford a full-time Cantor. At weddings also he would sing, at circumcisions, at Barmitzvahs, when boys became men. He was fat, and long past his best, and very popular indeed. Mark greeted him warmly and the meal was fun, with Sophie enjoying the old singer's stories as much as ever. Many she had heard before; but Berel had skill – and a most infectious laugh. He accepted with a delicate fat hand a glass of Sophie's cherry brandy.

'These days I choose my synagogues and weddings and celebrations more carefully,' he said. 'I try to avoid dentists, and dealers in horses. Doctors also. Cattlemen I like. And butchers.'

Sophie was intrigued. 'Why?' she asked.

Berel chuckled. 'Doctors and dentists and dealers in horses all give great attention to the mouth. Cattlemen and butchers base judgment on the weight, the *size*. At my age you look at – and listen to – yourself honestly. Eh, Mark?'

'It was never just for your voice,' said Mark gently. 'In any case, Sophie and I are not yet ready to weep for you. We hear tales of your singing in some very grand houses indeed. Perhaps not doctors or dentists, but of great timber merchants we've heard. A ship-owner, a property magnate.'

'Yes. Yes,' said Berel with a certain grandeur. 'But in such company I don't sing a note before I tell the little story.' He gave Sophie a raised eyebrow. 'You haven't heard the little story? Of God on the Eighth Day? When he was deciding the life-spans for his creatures?'

Sophie shook her head, entranced.

'First,' said Berel, 'the Dog, who asked what his life would be and how long. "To chew on bones," said God, "to howl at the moon, to belong to masters who will beat you if you disobey. Three score years and ten."

' "No thank you," said the Dog, "fifteen will be plenty."

' "As you wish," said God. "Next, Horse, who will pull heavy loads and be often whipped when tired. Three score years and ten."

' "Thirty will be ample," said the Horse. "Twenty-five even."

' "Very well," said God. "Now the Cantor. Who will sing in every kind of service and celebration in my name, who will have endless free food and drink and be always respected. Three score years and ten."

' "Longer!" cried the Cantor. "More! A wonderful life!"

'A problem for the Almighty,' said Berel. 'Where could he find extra years? Only from the Dog and the Horse. And this is why, Sophie my darling, as I tell everybody, you shouldn't be surprised if a Cantor, when he is old, sings like a dog and eats like a horse.'

8

The Rabbi was enjoying his evening. The Eve of Sabbath service had gone well and the synagogue had been nearly full. Now he was at home with a guest he was fond of. An unexpected guest, as always, for a matchmaker is a travelling man and can turn up anywhere, at any time.

His name was Motke and he sat across from Mark, smiling. They had eaten Sophie's excellent supper and the Rabbi had opened a bottle of his best wine. Sophie shared Mark's liking for this odd little man who always looked the same, in a black suit with a high wing-collar and silk cravat. Indoors now, he wore a skull-cap. His dusty top-hat and large umbrella he had laid aside. Motke, known far and wide, and respected. The talk at table had been splendid, with Sophie wiping tears of laughter more than once, for Motke had a true eye and words to tell of what he saw.

Motke put down his glass. 'As I have observed before in this house,' he said to Mark, 'our professions are similar, in many ways. Not easy, needing a great knowledge of people, careful judgment, delicate balance.'

'True,' said Mark, edging Motke towards another story. 'Delicate balance?'

'Delicate balance,' said the matchmaker firmly. 'Which can be upset in unforeseen ways by well-meaning persons causing great disturbance. Did I ever tell you of one of my greatest successes? A double success. The Innkeeper of Plotz? No? He was rich, with no sons and two daughters. One was ugly enough to frighten any man and the other, though better looking, was a shrew with a screech for a voice. He asked my help. A problem for Motke, you must agree.'

'Indeed,' replied Mark, who had heard the story but had an idea that he hadn't heard the *whole* story.

'The young women were not so young either,' said Motke. 'So I gave it careful thought. I took my time. Then came inspiration. Guidance from the Almighty. For the ugly one I found a blind man and for the screecher a deaf man.'

'You didn't!' exclaimed Sophie.

'Would I tell you a lie after such cooking?' said Motke. 'A double wedding, with a big dowry for each daughter and the innkeeper my friend for life. The couples prospered and lived in harmony. And why not? Motke had solved the problem. The years pass. And comes one day to

Plotz a great doctor said to perform great cures. The two husbands decide to consult him. Yes, he says, I can make *you* see and *you* hear. It will be costly. Do it, they say. And he does it. So now the blind one can see his ugly-as-sin wife and the deaf one can hear the all-day screeching. End of harmony. Great disturbance. Delicate balance destroyed. The husbands refuse to pay the doctor, saying he has done them great harm.'

'What happened?' asked Sophie, wide-eyed.

'It went to the court of Rabbi Joseph of Dubno who is a great sage. The Rabbi agreed with the husbands and told the doctor to make them as they were before. You never saw a doctor's bill paid so quickly.'

'A great judgment,' said Mark.

'A great story,' said Sophie.

'A great interference in my good work!' said Motke.

9

It was not often that the Rabbi left the little town of Klaneshtetl. Even more rarely did he travel by train. The nearest station was far away. But when he did go anywhere on a train he always enjoyed it. He would be provisioned with tasty snacks by Sophie, who would also see that nothing in his appearance suggested his calling. 'The Cossacks play very rough with Rabbis,' she would say.

So there sat Mark, in his quiet observant fashion, food-basket on knees, in the corner of the carriage, which was full. The talk overlapped and the Rabbi enjoyed it all. He sat next to a portly man dressed in expensive clothes, with fine boots and a heavy gold ring on his finger. A young man, opposite, leant forward and tapped the rich man's knee. 'Can you tell me the time?' he asked, 'I don't have a watch.' No reply. 'I'm going to Lublin,' said the young man. 'First time, to look for work.'

'If you're going to Lublin,' said the rich man, 'not only will I not tell you the time but I don't wish to talk to you at all.'

The young man was flabbergasted. Mark waited.

'Nothing personal,' said the rich man to the carriage. 'I tell him the time. A word leads to another, the weather, politics, this and that. I live in Lublin, he's going to Lublin. It's only right I take him home for a meal, a bed. He meets my daughter, who is the apple of my eye. They fall in love. Do you think I would let my daughter marry somebody without a job – who doesn't even own a watch!'

The carriage went back to its papers. Mark smiled at the young man, who smiled back. Soon, from behind two of the papers:

'Did you do what I suggested about your insomnia?'

'The counting of the sheep? Yes, I did. Are you mad, suggesting such a thing?'

'What are you talking about? An ancient remedy. It didn't work?'

'Ten times worse. I counted sheep. Soon I have ten thousand sheep. From the wool I get enough material for thirty-five hundred coats. The whole night I'm lying there worrying where I can get linings and buttons for thirty-five hundred coats!'

Mark gave the young man a sandwich.

From behind another two papers:

'You know Livitch? Who never pays his bills?'

'I know him. He's cost me plenty.'

'Me too. He told me yesterday that the more he likes a person the more he haggles over the price.'

'Why, for God's sake, if he's not going to pay anyway?'

'He said he doesn't like his friend's bad debts to be too big.'

An old woman gave the young man an apple. 'Eat,' she said. 'Eat, and don't worry. You don't need his daughter, you'll find another girl. And please God you'll have a married life as happy as mine was. Forty years, with never a penny to spare. Eight children. All well. Brought up on nothing. Poverty. Every week a few coppers for the insurance man. Seven weeks ago suddenly I'm a widow. I tell the insurance man and suddenly I'm rich. Well, that's life. If my Sam had lived a little longer he could have shared it with me.'

The Rabbi settled himself. It was going to be a good journey.

10

The Rabbi was a bit tired. The week had been busy, busier even than usual, for it had included one of the minor Feast Days with its special Service, a wedding, and also a funeral. Now it was Sunday and Mark was enjoying the quiet of his own small house. Sophie had given him a fine lunch, with a glass or two of wine and they had talked of this and that and they had shared the washing-up. Now Mark was drowsy, and so was Sophie. The little parlour was warm, and very peaceful.

There was a loud knocking on the door, and Sophie went to see who it was. Mark could hear her voice but not the words. There was a sharp note in her voice. Most unusual, thought Mark sleepily, settling himself for a nap. Then Sophie was back, looking cross.

'It's the Cockerel men,' she said, pink with exasperation. 'They say you promised them a Rabbinic judgment after "further thought and consultation". They won't go away.'

Mark groaned, and sat up. 'Show them in,' he said. 'And go up and rest.'

'I'll stay,' said Sophie firmly. 'You need rest more than I do and those two idiots will waste your whole afternoon. What "further thought and consultation"?'

'It was half a joke, to make them stop pestering me,' said Mark weakly.

'You and your jokes,' said Sophie, and went out. After a moment she ushered two men into the room. She sat them down opposite Mark and sat herself next to Mark, looking legal and straight-backed.

'I act today,' she announced, 'as "fresh ear" in this matter, as suggested in the methods of further thought used in modern jurisprudence.'

The men blinked. So did Mark, but he felt humour returning. He glanced at Sophie but she looked ahead, at the two men.

Mark paused, studying the men. They were very different, sharing only an obstinate angry expression. They sat apart, with set mouths, waiting. One was thin and pale, very grey and dusty in looks, with claw-like hands and bent shoulders. Watery eyes, and a sharp beak for a nose.

The other was square, peasant-heavy, with thick clothes and big boots. His face was broad, with not much colour. Very bald, except for untidy yellowy wisps.

Both were scholars, both widowers, both (it

46

was said) of sufficient means to support their endless (and some would say pointless) studies of the mystical books of the Ancients. They lived next door to each other.

'Let me,' said Mark, 'briefly recapitulate for my wife, the Rebbitzen, acting today as fresh ear. Please feel free to correct any inaccuracy.'

The two men nodded grimly.

'On a certain date last year,' said Mark to yellowy-wisps, whose name was Wispitch, 'you bought a cockerel, liking its appearance and finding its early morning noise "agreeable and stimulating to thought and study". Your own words, I believe?' Another grim nod. 'It came to your attention that your neighbour, Mr – er – Graydek' (from the grey one a nod, as grim), 'was taking advantage of the cockerel's early-morning noise also, to rise early and begin *his* studies, fully awakened and alert. You then approached Mr Graydek suggesting that as he shared the benefits of the cockerel's early-morning noise he should also share in its upkeep. He did not agree and you have brought this serious matter before me some four times.'

'Five,' said Wispitch.

'Five,' said Mark. 'And we have discussed at considerable length and in great detail all the arguments put forth by both parties. Ownership of the cockerel is not in dispute. Nor is the fact that the cockerel's voice is heard by both parties. Neither party is deaf and the cockerel's voice is loud and clear.'

47

Mark and Sophie dared not look at each other. 'It would seem, therefore,' said the Rabbi, in most Rabbinic tones, 'that what must be decided here is: for whom does the cock crow?' He let the silence go on for a while. 'For the final judgment and consultation please pay to the fresh ear twenty-five roubles each.'

The men were startled but Mark's stern face forbade argument and they gave Sophie the money.

'Hear now the judgment,' intoned Mark. 'The cock crows neither for *you* nor for *you*. It crows for *me*! For I have just taken fifty roubles to help poor children from two idiots who have wasted my time on five different occasions – *and* are keeping me from my after-lunch sleep. *Go home*!'

He rose, his face like thunder, and the men fled. Sophie closed the front door after them and came back, in tears of laughter.

'Why didn't you do it weeks ago?' she said, kissing him.

'It needed a fresh ear,' said Mark.

11

It was the day of the month when Mark put
aside his Rabbi's hat and put on the hat of
the magistrate. In the old days, the days we
speak of, the Rabbi of a small town like Klaneshtetl did many jobs, and presiding over a small
Rabbinic court was one. Mark was aware of the
responsibility but quite enjoyed it on occasion.

Today had been rather dull. Petty things,
which should never have come to court. As so
often in the past Mark wondered at the amount
of heat caused by small aggravations.

It was mid-afternoon. Now Mark was to hear
the case of Tevye the Innkeeper and Mishkin
the Scholar, who again had drunk far more than
he could pay for. Mark didn't expect to hear
anything new (it wasn't the first time), but he was
fond of Mishkin, who had a certain wit, and the
Rabbi was always drawn to humour.

He listened first to the innkeeper, who indeed
had nothing new to say about Mishkin, who was

a persuasive chap in the matter of getting his thirst quenched.

Mishkin too had little to say that was different. 'Guilty, Rabbi,' he said. 'Guilty. I'll find some work, earn some money, and pay the bill. I'm sorry. Guilty and sorry. I was sad, so I went to the inn. I drank not so much to assuage thirst as to drown my sorrows.'

'And did they drown, your sorrows?' asked Mark.

'No,' said Mishkin. 'They have become good swimmers.' He kept a straight face, and so did Mark; but both knew it was time for one of the little exchanges they enjoyed so much. Mark sat forward.

'I have no note of sorrow or sadness,' he said. 'The opposite in fact. Singing and dancing, it says here. Jokes. A party. You have education, and words. Explain.'

'I was renewed and refreshed by the first drink,' said Mishkin. 'A new man. I liked him, the new man, so I bought *him* a drink. Soon we were seeing more than one of each other – and no one was left out! After all, we were very close. Related, happy in each other's company. And as the Talmud says, where happiness is, it is permitted to drink. So we drank. Had I been by myself perhaps I would not have taken so much.'

Mark blinked, and smiled. The day was saved. 'You used to have students,' he said. 'You were a teacher. Then you became, shall we say, a wine-taster.'

'A taster of wine first,' said Mishkin, '*Then* a teacher. I taught to be able to extend my knowledge of the grape. Who knows, a professorship, a doctorate. Such research takes money, so I taught.'

'Perhaps,' said Mark, 'if you gave up drinking your pupils would return.'

Mishkin drew himself up. A lecturer with bloodshot eyes. 'I must ask you, Rabbi,' he stated, 'to listen more carefully. I have explained that for years I taught so that I could drink. Are you now seriously suggesting that I should give up drink so that I can teach? Is your judgment slipping? Have you no sense of priorities?'

'Forgive me,' said Mark humbly. 'Perhaps you could now offer instruction based on your vast knowledge of the fruits of the vine. The arts of the vintner and so on.'

'Impossible,' said Mishkin. 'Practical demonstration would be essential, which would be unwise.'

'For your pupils?' said Mark.

'Of course,' said Mishkin, 'who else?'

12

It was the Rabbi's habit to listen carefully when Sophie gave voice to something on her mind. Not that he didn't always listen with courtesy but they'd been married a long time and there's listening and listening.

'Mark,' said Sophie, 'you know the big heavy parcel of books and stuff that came over from the next village this morning whilst you were at the synagogue?'

'Yes,' said Mark, finishing his lunch.

'It didn't come horse and cart,' said Sophie. 'It was carried! By a not very young man either.'

'Well,' said Mark, 'there are carters and there are men who carry. Not all men who deliver have carts and horses.'

'He used to have a horse and cart,' Sophie went on. 'And more. And more. He told me about himself when I gave him a sandwich and tea. He talked to me.'

Mark smiled. His Sophie was a woman with

time for people. From Sophie a person would get a sandwich, tea *and* sympathy. Sophie was someone you could talk to. Everybody talked to Sophie.

'Do you know,' said Sophie, 'that man used to be *rich*. Not rich like here in Klaneshtetl, but *real* rich. An estate, a great house, with servants and carriages. A great business, employing many. Don't give me that look, Mark, I know when somebody's lying. He wasn't.'

'What happened?' said Mark.

'Everything,' said Sophie. 'Bad partners, bad luck, bankruptcy, disaster. All he had left was a tiny cottage and a bit of garden. He made the cottage into a little shop and managed. Then again bad luck. The cottage burnt down and with it all he possessed. Poor man. Dreadful.'

'And then?' asked Mark.

'So he had to sell the bit of land of the cottage and he bought a horse and cart and became a carter. They hardly had enough to eat. After all, in a carter's family, the horse is a mouth to feed. The biggest mouth. Thank God we don't have a horse. You should give thanks every day you're a Rabbi, Mark, and not a carter.'

'I do,' said Mark solemnly. 'Every day. What happened to the horse and cart?'

'The horse died,' said Sophie, near to tears. 'Perhaps you could help him, Mark. A word of comfort; a friendly hand. Next time he comes through.'

Mark promised, and waited. A week passed

53

and he saw the man resting on the bench outside
Sophie's kitchen. Sophie made tea and a sandwich and Mark took it out. He was tentative and
tactful, and the man, after a sharp glance,
accepted him. This was no pack-slave, this man.

Sophie looked out. 'Tell him,' she said to the
man. 'He's my husband.'

Mark listened again to the man's tale. He noted
a complete lack of complaint in the man. Even a
grim humour.

'Wonderful days you've known,' said Mark. 'An estate, a mansion, carriages, servants, riches. Wonderful days. Do you ever want them back?'

The man laughed. 'Not for a minute, Rabbi. What I really want back are those wonderful days when I had a horse and cart.' He laughed again.

So did Mark. In admiration.

13

In the twenty-five years that Mark had been the Rabbi in the little town of Klaneshtetl he had learnt far more than he had taught – and knew it. His parishioners were a very mixed bunch and needed a lot of patience and skill. They could be very irritating indeed. 'Not all of them,' Mark would say to Sophie. 'Not the young and the old. It's that middle lot.'

For the very old Mark had special affection, for the dozen or so old men who were in the little synagogue every morning for the early service and who stayed on to discuss things, to argue, to doze off near the stove. 'My Temple Elders,' Mark would call them, and when he could spare time he would stay on with them, just to listen, and chuckle.

This morning, a chilly morning of sudden showers, old Fyvel had arrived late, holding things up, for a quorum was needed before a service could start and he was the tenth. He'd come in soaked, umbrella in hand.

'Why didn't you use your umbrella?' Mark asked, concerned.

'I did. I did,' said Fyvel. 'It's old, full of holes.'

'Why did you have it with you?' said Mark.

'I didn't think it would rain,' said Fyvel.

The other Elders had nodded in perfect understanding. They put Fyvel by the stove to dry and began the service. After, they stayed. It was cosy and also there were things to talk about. In particular the matter of the stolen poor-box. Thief unknown and no clues, not that the old men wanted to catch and punish. To replace was more important, so that charity and the giving of alms should not be interrupted.

'The new box is ready,' announced Potchik, who was nearly the eldest, and a respected voice. 'But this time we will fix it to the ceiling, where no robber can reach it. A good solution, yes?'

This wisdom was applauded. 'How,' asked old Fyvel, with steam still rising from him, 'how, if the box is on the ceiling, will people be able to put money in?'

A good point. It was considered carefully, old fingers combing through beards.

'A ladder,' proclaimed Potchik at last. 'A ladder, for the use of the charitable. Available at all times. Molik will lend his ladder from his orchard. Eh, Molik?'

Molik nodded. 'But the ladder is old and unsteady,' he said. 'It takes skill. On soft earth, yes. On a level floor, very dangerous. A person could fall. The charitable should not be put at risk. It is not right.'

Here was also wisdom. Again the old heads nodded and gave thought. It was very quiet. Mark waited. These moments for him were beyond price.

This time it was Zelman, the oldest of them all, who spoke. A true sage.

'A new ladder. Of a kind easy to climb and with a handrail. And to avoid all risk to the charitable it should be secured strongly to both floor and ceiling.'

There was a feeling of contentment and happiness in the little synagogue. Another problem solved. Ah, the wisdom of old age.

Mark nodded with the Elders, enchanted, in full agreement. He considered whether he should point out something, but decided it could wait.

14

The Rabbi was on his way back to Klaneshtetl. For four days he had been in a larger, more prosperous town in the western part of the province. He had been filling in for a friend, who was ill. Among the duties he had performed for his friend had been two funerals, on following days. The first of them was that of a rich man, famous for his loose-living, his profligacy, his huge appetites for everything. A gambler, a womanizer, a prankster on a grand scale.

The second funeral was also of a rich man. A scholar, an ascetic who rarely left his study, a man of iron discipline who ate only vegetables and drank only water. Who wrote long articles in foreign languages about remote subjects, understood only by others like him in far-off places. Positively the town's most distinguished resident.

Rabbi Mark had known neither man and was puzzled; for at the loose-living lecher's funeral the whole town had gathered, to weep and mourn and wail, whilst to that of the town's most famous scholar no one but family had come. People as stiff and remote and dry as the scholar was said to have been. A puzzle, thought Mark, as he alighted from the coach at the stop nearest to Klaneshtetl. The coachman whipped up the horses, and Mark was alone. He picked up his bag and walked. It was a fine late afternoon. He looked forward to the dinner Sophie would have ready – and to seeing his Sophie, from whom he did not like to be parted. But this of the two funerals, very strange. Certainly the gambler had had many cronies and hangers-on, even some real old friends, but the whole *town*? He changed the bag to the other hand.

'Put the bag on the barrow, Rabbi,' said a cheerful voice. 'Yourself too if you're tired.'

It was Isaac the Beggar, an old friend. Mark was grateful to be free of the bag. He fell into step with Isaac, who said, 'You were far away, Rabbi. Big worries?'

Mark chuckled. 'Not really. Isaac, you go all over the province and know everybody; let me tell you of two funerals that puzzle me.'

Isaac listened carefully, then looked sideways at Mark and grinned. 'No mystery, Rabbi. I was acquainted with both parties. The whole town mourns the big-spender because he benefited the whole town. Everybody; the tailors, butchers, bakers, those who sold fish and wine and every good thing for the table. He supported actors and singers and musicians. Single-handed almost he gave work enough for three midwives – *and* looked after the mothers. He lived and laughed and paid a fair price for good value. A benefactor, a prince! As for the other feller, of what profit is a dry stick who no one sees – who eats only vegetables and drinks water? Who will miss such a man? Who will notice he is gone? Priorities, Rabbi! Correct values! Honour given where deserved! Eh, Rabbi, eh?'

'Join us for dinner,' said Mark.

'Delighted,' said the Beggar.

15

The Rabbi walked home for the little lunch Sophie made for him each day. He was feeling at peace, and a bit amused too. For the gossip in the market had all been about Blindl the Miser, who it seems had been having some bad turns lately, and feeling poorly. Someone had told of how the tight-fisted old man had gone to a well-known physician who charged a high fee for the first consultation and much less for the subsequent ones. 'Ah, Doctor,' said Blindl, first-timer, 'here I am again. Same trouble. For check up.' After examination, the Doctor, no fool, said, 'No change, really. Carry on as before. Same treatment.'

But now, it seemed, Blindl was a bit scared too, in a way not new to Mark, who'd seen many people change their ways in old age, as the Day of Judgment (whether you believed in it or not) came nearer.

Sophie, when he told her, laughed out loud.

'That beastly old man,' she said. 'That explains the note and the donation.'

'From whom?' asked Mark.

'From Blindl!' said Sophie. ' "A small donation," he writes, "to assist the less fortunate. It can be announced in synagogue. Five roubles. Anonymous. From Mr Blindl." '

Mark laughed. 'Five roubles! A day's food for a family. But from a man who's never given a penny in his whole life, munificent. There's a sermon in it somewhere, I'm positive of it.'

'There's five roubles in it and nothing else,' said Sophie crossly, practically. 'Don't be so happy with it, Mark. The man's got thousands!' She went quiet then and gave Mark his lunch, looking a bit thoughtful, with every now and then the little smile of pure mischief that Mark found enchanting.

He spent the afternoon at the synagogue and made some visits on the way home.

'Supper in the parlour tonight,' said Sophie. 'Not the kitchen. A celebration.' Mark didn't argue for the smells coming from the kitchen were Sophie at her best. A lot of cheerful humming too from Sophie. Mark read a little and drank a glass of wine. 'All ready,' sang Sophie, and led the way into the parlour. The table was laid prettily. The centrepiece a bowl of gold coins, with a yellow rose stuck in the middle.

Mark blinked. 'Eat first,' said Sophie.

The meal was splendid.

'Speak,' said Mark.

'I visited Blindl,' said Sophie. 'To thank him for his kind donation, to drink a glass of tea with him, whilst he talked of his aches and pains – and to tell him an ancient legend.'

'Would I know the legend?' asked Mark.

'Well, it's not *that* ancient,' said Sophie. 'I made it up on my way to Blindl's.'

'Continue,' said Mark. 'I collect ancient legends.'

'It's about the mean wicked old skinflint,' said Sophie, 'who died and found himself down below in Hell being prepared and kitted out for ever-lasting torment and slow burning. Demons were checking over his rotten and selfish life. "Not a single charitable act," pronounced the chief clerk.

' "Wait!" screamed the miser, "Once I gave five roubles to a poor man. Long ago. I swear it! It can be proved."

' "Wait," said the chief clerk and sent a message up to the chief clerk of Heaven, who went into it. His reply was brief. "The gentleman is known to us and is found wanting. Kindly return to him the enclosed five roubles. Inform him that membership fees here were *never* that low." '

16

The visits of the Government Inspector to Klaneshtetl were never occasions to be anticipated with pleasure or remembered with fondness. The Inspectors were chosen for their hardness and an affection for Jews was not regarded as a good thing. The little town was always apprehensive before a visit and in a state of nervous relief after. Inspectors were men of great power, and hand-in-glove it was said with the feared marauding Cossacks. A person had to be careful with the tongue, to show respect, to show clearly to the Inspector that a small-town Jew *was* inferior in every way to His Excellency.

The Rabbi had had dealings over the years with a number of different Inspectors. In training and attitude they had been the same. They were promoted or retired, and a new one would appear. Today's was a new one, and Mark observed him closely. To know the enemy was not only intelligent but part of his duty to his flock, for as

Rabbi he was always present during questionings or examinings, and could act as buffer or shield, or expert on certain community matters.

As hard as any of them, thought Mark. With a vain look, and no humour at all, which gave him a little misgiving, for certain people in the town had as quick an eye for the official who could be fooled as he had.

The little hall next to the synagogue was fairly full. The Inspector sat at a long trestle table looking through his files. His aide, of similar appearance and uniform, sat at one end. It was quiet, mid-morning. There had been few words exchanged between the Rabbi and the Inspector, who disliked Jews in general and Rabbis in particular.

Without looking up the Inspector said: 'I understand that in the town of Bilyowitz there are neither pigs nor Jews.'

'It would seem a place,' said Mark respectfully, 'for us *both* to visit.'

The Inspector's head came up sharply but Mark had his blandest face ready. The Inspector chose a folder.

'Tailor Schneider,' he rapped.

'Step forward,' intoned the aide. 'Stand to attention. Cap off. Answer clearly, without lies.'

Schneider, small and thin, with a bent back, stood cap in hand, with his eyes steady and unafraid. Mark tensed. The tailor was no fool, and in his long feud with Grobbek the Butcher had shown a ready tongue and considerable wit.

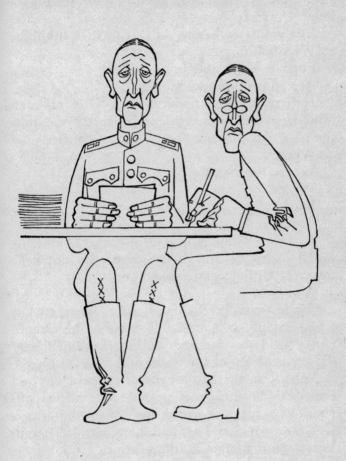

'Arrested by the police this year I see,' said the Inspector. 'Questioned, kept in jail overnight, fined. Correct?'

'Yes, your Excellency,' said Schneider, humbly.

'What for?'

'For not being able to swim.'

'Are you trying to be funny?'

'Indeed not, your Excellency. One of your military colleagues accidentally threw me into the river, kicking me first, in fun of course.'

'Where?'

'Where the kick?'

'Where the river.'

'Polyntz.'

'Continue.'

'I cannot swim. I was drowning. Your honoured colleague and *his* colleague did not hear my cries for help and walked on.'

'And then?'

'Then, your Excellency, hardly knowing what I was saying, I shouted "God curse the Czar!" and your two esteemed colleagues immediately dragged me out of the water and arrested me.'

Nobody in the hall moved or spoke. Here and there the beginning of a smile was wiped off. Mark kept his eyes on the Inspector, who after a long moment closed the folder, saying, 'Very well. Watch your tongue in future.'

'As though my very life depended on it,' promised Schneider.

As the Inspector sorted his files, he said, 'I call my dog Isaac.'

'A Jewish name,' said Mark, as expected to.

'Well, he's a Jew-dog,' said the Inspector.

'A handicap, such a name,' said Mark, 'with a different name, who knows, the dog could become an Inspector. Of dogs.' As the hard eyes came up he had a silly smile ready. Again the silence in the hall except for a chuckle immediately turned into a violent cough.

'Shoichet Grobbek,' said the Inspector.

'Step forward,' said the aide. 'Stand to attention. Cap off. Answer clearly, without lies.'

The big butcher walked forward, his face red with anger. Mark was worried. Grobbek was a man of violent temper, bull-like, full of self-importance. In this situation, dangerous to the town.

'Shoichet Grobbek?' said the Inspector. 'Application for slaughter licence received ten days late. Form incorrectly completed –'

'*Shoichet* Grobbek?' said Grobbek. 'What *Shoichet*? My name is *Mister* Grobbek.'

The Inspector examined the file.

'Name: Grobbek,' he said coldly. 'Trade: Slaughterer. In your own foul tongue, Shoichet. Shoichet Grobbek. Perfectly in order.'

The veins in the butcher's neck swelled. Mark offered up a silent prayer. Grobbek looked from one side to the other. A bull. His eyes met those of his arch-enemy, the tailor, whose own eyes were a little concerned. Grobbek caught the concern and steadied himself, taking calmness (and inspiration too, some said later) from Schneider.

'Your Excellency,' said Grobbek, with great deliberation, 'in addition to being a Schoichet I am also a householder. And in addition to being a householder I am also a Warden in synagogue.' His voice took on the sing-song of Rabbinic conclusion. 'So when I stand in front of my neighbours: *Mister* Grobbek. When I am standing in front of the congregation: *Warden* Grobbek. But when I am standing in front of a stupid ox . . .'

The violent coughing in the little hall was terrible to hear.

17

'A message,' said Sophie to the Rabbi as he came in. 'From Mitchik the Lawyer. Can he see you for a few minutes after supper. It's important. I said yes, was I right?'

The Rabbi kissed his wife. It had been a busy day, and sad too, for an old friend, Kotcher of the Wine-shop, was coming to the end of his life. 'Of course,' he said. 'Mitchik doesn't waste my time.'

'It's about Kotcher of the Wine-shop,' said Sophie. 'About a will. Come and eat, you look washed out.'

The lawyer arrived and was direct. 'Did Kotcher strike you as of sound mind when you saw him last?' he said.

'Absolutely,' said Mark. 'As always. I was with him three days ago. Ill, yes; old too, but solid as a rock. Why?'

'His will,' said Mitchik. 'You know his sons?' Mark knew them, men in their late thirties. One as wild as the other was quiet. The elder, the wild one, a gambler and drinker, a spender who ran up huge debts. The younger a studious, steady person. A great help in his father's various businesses, of which the wine-shop was only one.

'All the businesses and farms to the wild one,' said Mitchik. 'The wine-shop alone to the steady one. Sound mind?'

Mark was startled. His old friend had built a considerable fortune with great foresight. Foresight. 'A mistake?' he said. 'Checked over? Was it pointed out?'

'Every word checked; every paragraph initialled,' said the lawyer. 'He won't discuss it, or accept advice. Could you go and see him, Mark? I'm worried.'

Mark was too, and promised. He went the next day and was shown in by Ben, the younger son, who looked sad, for the end was not far off now.

Old Kotcher was pleased to see Mark. 'Come,' he said, 'sit close, and smile. Be pleased for me. All is arranged and tidy. I have no complaints. Soon I will be with my darling Nina, who has had eight years to prepare our home up there.' He chuckled, and the two friends were easy together.

Mark carefully worked round to the lawyer's concern. The old man looked at Mark with amused and very sensible eyes.

'No need for concern,' he said. 'No mistake. My wine-shop is the only one in town and the best in the district. My wild one has squandered a fortune there. When I am gone he will be very wealthy. He and his friends will gamble and drink away all the businesses and the farms too. In the wine-shop. All the debts will be to the wine-shop, to his brother, who eventually will own everything and look after it well until my wild one changes. As he will, for I was wilder than him at his age and I changed. It is not foresight, my good friend, it is an honest memory. A man should recall himself with truth, and not hate in his child what he recognizes of himself.'

He was quiet for a while with his eyes closed. Mark waited, aware of having been taught a lesson, and grateful. The old man opened one eye. 'This is a thing for Rabbis to understand,' he said, 'not lawyers.'

18

It was again the day of the month when the meeting-hall next door to the synagogue in Klaneshtetl became a courtroom and the Rabbi became a Judge. It was one of his duties and he didn't complain. The little town's disputes and wrangles were best aired and cleared away and Mark's quiet common sense was widely respected.

The morning's cases had been of a kind requiring no Solomon, and Mark had been home for a bowl of soup with Sophie, who wanted to come to court for the afternoon. A friend was in trouble. Mark's friend too, Isaac the Beggar, to whom trouble was no stranger. Indeed, trouble in the form of sickness in his youngest child had led him into this trouble. 'It's not that I want to make sure you judge the matter fairly,' said Sophie to her husband. 'I want to make sure you keep a straight face. You and Isaac are a pair.'

They went back through the market, taking

some carrots for the small herd of donkeys that people hired to carry themselves and their goods up and over the hill to the next town, Lodditch. 'Are the donkeys to be in court, as evidence?' asked Sophie.

The court was crowded. 'All plaintiffs,' said Mark softly. 'Not too many taking it seriously I see. Good.' He took his seat in the big chair. Bang-bang with the gavel.

'Who speaks for the plaintiffs?' asked Mark.

Nathan the Pawnbroker rose. Sharp nose, a spokesman sort of voice, no humour at all.

Mark looked across at the beggar, who stood at ease with his usual shrewd unworried look. 'Begin,' said Mark.

'The market-day before last,' said Nathan, 'Isaac rushed into the space near the donkeys and cracked a big whip. He said he would take us to Lodditch for one third the usual price and half an hour before the usual time. He took our money, gave it to his middle son to take to the doctor or some such and told us to follow him, which we did.'

'On the donkeys?' asked Mark.

'No. On foot,' said Nathan edgily. 'We thought perhaps he had other donkeys, up the hill. He led us, walking fast, cracking the whip. At the top of the hill, no donkeys. He walked on, not listening to us. What could we do? Top of the hill is half-way. Soon we were in Lodditch. No donkeys. Swindled. A clear case. Money back and prison, nothing less.'

'Thank you,' said Mark. 'Isaac?'

The beggar looked around, carefully avoiding Mark's eye. Sophie's too. 'I said I would take you all to Lodditch, yes? For one third the usual price. Yes? And right away immediately after receipt of money. Yes? Which I did. Yes?'

'Answer please,' said Mark in his Judge voice. The crowd did not argue.

'Who said anything about donkeys?' said Isaac. 'Did I say one word about donkeys?'

A woman began to laugh. Mark was relieved. Nathan fumed and spluttered. 'The whole way,' he shouted. 'I looked around. Not a single donkey!'

'Look around now,' said Isaac. 'You'll see nothing *but* donkeys.' There was a roar of laughter, from everyone. He looked at Mark, straight-faced. 'Case dismissed, Rabbi?'

'Yes, I think so,' said Mark. 'How's the little one, better?'

'Yes, thank you,' said Isaac.

19

As the Rabbi prepared for bed he felt happy. It had been a good day. With an unusual ending which had added salt. It had begun during the morning. He had glanced out of the window of his little office above the synagogue and at first hadn't believed his eyes. A priest in the Russian Orthodox long black robe and cylindrical hat, but covered in mud and decidedly unsteady on his feet! The priest turned the corner and Mark went on with his work, puzzled, for he knew the priest of Klaneshtetl well. In a small town you know everybody. A short round man, not the big shambling chap he'd just seen.

When Mark got home he told his wife of his day, as always. Sophie listened and then laughed. 'You weren't seeing things,' she said. 'It was Mischa the Drunkard.'

Mark knew him well. A nice man who'd gone to pieces when his wife died and whose only child, a daughter, had later run off with a soldier to the other end of Russia. A nice man. A peasant, who'd never gone to school. A farm-worker once, and respected, but now the town drunk and a butt for all sorts of rough jokes.

'How come the priest's clothes?' asked Mark.

'Some students from the Catholic College in the next town found him in a ditch,' replied Sophie, 'and they took away his own clothes and dressed him up. He was dead drunk. It was last night. He didn't wake up till this morning. The whole town is laughing behind their hands but treating him like a priest. You don't think it funny, Mark?'

'Yes and no,' said Mark, and Sophie, who was wise, got on with cooking the meal.

After they'd eaten, Mark put his feet up and read a book. Suddenly Sophie was in from the kitchen.

'It's Mischa!' she said. 'He's out the back. He wants to see you.'

'Front parlour,' said Mark. 'Bring him through. Make some strong coffee.'

Mischa looked terrible. Unshaven, dirty, still in his priest's clothes, and very in need of a friend.

The big man blinked away a tear or two. Gathered his thoughts, which took time. Started to speak once or twice and then paused. Mark waited.

'At first,' said Mischa, 'at first when I woke up I thought it was one of my drunk-dreams which can be terrible. Then I knew the clothes were real. I felt them, I pulled at them. Real, with a

78

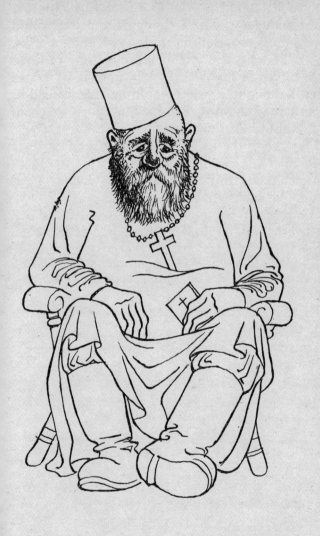

hat. So I thought maybe I've been turned into a priest somehow. No, I thought, a priest would have a cross round his neck. Look, Rabbi, a cross. No, I thought, a priest would have one of those little bibles in his pocket. And here it is! Look! Then I thought, a priest would be able to read it. I can't read a word, Rabbi. Surely a priest can *read*, Rabbi? Can *you* read?'

Mark took the little bible and looked hard. 'I can't read very well,' he said.

Mischa was full of wonder. 'So I *could* be a priest,' he said. 'Like you, Rabbi.'

'You could be anything you wanted to be,' replied Mark, as Sophie came in. 'Have some coffee.'

20

In a small town like Klaneshtetl people live close to each other and know perhaps too much about others. Likes and dislikes are inclined to be a bit stronger. Rabbi Mark observed all this and it gave him as much amusement as aggravation. For weeks now he had been watching Grobbek, the loud-voiced tactless butcher who was built like a wrestler, and Schneider the tailor, who was small and bent and gentle, and who irritated Grobbek exceedingly. It had begun when the tailor had gone to the butcher, who was treasurer of the Burial Society, for money to bury his wife.

'What's this!' the butcher had roared, in front of everybody. 'You already *had* money to bury your wife, two years ago!'

'This is another wife,' said Schneider sadly.

'You married *again*?' shouted Grobbek, who'd known, but liked to make jokes. 'Congratulations!'

Schneider had made no reply, had taken the few roubles and buried his wife. He had a quiet sort of humour, had the tailor, and was patient. The bull-like Grobbek began to find the tailor under his feet, cropping up, popping out. Always with a polite word or a remark that the butcher was never quite certain meant what it sounded like.

Once, in the cemetery, Grobbek was paying due respect at the burial of a very rich man. The family stood weeping. Suddenly by Grobbek's side stood Schneider, also weeping.

'What, are you a relative?' asked the butcher.

'In no way,' said the tailor.

'Then why do you weep?' said Grobbek.

'That's why,' said Schneider, and walked softly away.

There were many such moments and Mark heard about them all. 'The tailor is a little ahead,' he told Sophie his wife. 'But Grobbek can be very crude and rough. I think he's cooking something up.'

'My money's on the tailor,' said Sophie. 'He's faster on his feet.'

It happened on the next Sabbath. Most people in Klaneshtetl had a Sabbath coat and most of the coats had been made by Schneider, who was a fine craftsman, but whose prices were so low that he remained a poor man, who worked long hours, single-handed. Schneider's own coat was a disgrace – worn every day, Sabbath too.

'A disgrace!' roared Grobbek in front of everybody, as the service ended. 'An insult to the Almighty, such a coat! You should be ashamed!' Schneider hung his head. Grobbek's voice grew louder. 'Tomorrow, my friends, I will give the tailor out of my own pocket twenty roubles, nearly the price of a new coat, for him to renovate his own disgusting coat so that he can mix with decent people without shame. This Grobbek does for Schneider!'

The next Sabbath, the tailor was the last to arrive in synagogue, some minutes after the service had begun, his coat unchanged. Grobbek went purple. People smiled into their prayer-books and could hardly wait for the service to end. Neither could Mark, cutting his sermon to the bone.

Schneider spoke clearly, heard by everybody. 'I costed the repair-work on my coat very carefully. Had I done it for that money I would have lost heavily on it. So I made a little coat for my granddaughter. Red velvet, with white buttons. From the butcher, I told her.' The little tailor looked around. 'This Schneider does for Grobbek,' he said.

21

The Rabbi had great affection for the old men of the synagogue, his 'Temple Elders', and they had the same feelings for him, and great loyalty also, both to him and their religion, for no service could begin 'unless ten were present' and ten there always were. Rain or shine, hot or cold, in sickness or in health, there would always be a quorum. Mark respected the old men as much as he found amusement in them, for they discussed and dissected everything in the many hours they spent in the little house of prayer. It was their club, their refuge. After a service, if Mark had time, he would stay on, content to listen, to not speak till spoken to, to chuckle to himself at the strange conclusions arrived at, the involved reasonings and weighings-up.

Sadly, this morning he could not spare the time. He'd left the oldsters round the stove and had come up to his little office. There was paperwork to be done, which was boring but could not be avoided. Klaneshtetl, like any other small town, had to give careful account of itself to the Authorities, the provincial government, which had great power and no great love for its Jewish citizens. Reports had to be regularly submitted; forms returned, questionnaires completed. It took patience and care. He worked steadily.

His door opened an inch or two. It was old Fyvel, who was vague and gentle.

'We don't like to disturb you, Rabbi, but it is a matter of some importance to the town. If you can spare a few minutes. Very important. We are happy to come up if you don't wish to leave your desk.'

Mark put down his pen. This was most unusual. The old men never intruded; never came up. It wasn't just tact. The stairs were steep and uneven and their legs were old and stiff.

'I'll come down,' said Mark.

The old men were quiet as he joined them. He waited, sensing something special in the air. Old Potchik spoke first, breaking the ice, leading up to the matter, sort of.

'We have been discussing the coming of the Messiah, Rabbi,' he said. 'To some it could represent great disturbance, great disruption.'

'Can you explain?' said Mark, to get this preamble out of the way, for he could see that the others were waiting, their eyes upon him. This of the Messiah had been talked about a thousand times.

'Well,' said Potchik, 'all we know is that there will be great changes. What *kind* of changes we don't know. We have lived long, have seen many things, have become settled in our ways. We live quietly, keeping the peace. We have established our families, done our best. If great change comes, who knows what can happen?'

Nathan the Pawnbroker obviously also wanted to get to the main question. He was sharp.

'We have survived many terrible things in this town. Drought, flood, pogroms and persecutions, taxes and fines, death and destruction. God helped us live through it. When the Messiah comes God will help us live through that also.'

'I'm sure he will,' said Mark. 'Was that the matter of importance? It could have waited perhaps.'

There was a little silence. One or two wheezy clearing of throats. Then old Klapyov spoke:

'Certainly the coming of the Messiah is not unimportant, although, as you say, not *urgent*. We would speak to you upon the matter of the Baker and the Army Flour.'

Mark's attention sharpened. One of his questionnaires upstairs had to do with this. A bad business. The town's baker, Yeltov, had bought flour from a catering sergeant in the army. The man had been caught and had given names. The hearing was next week. An examining officer was to come to the town and take Yeltov away to prison, for he was guilty. No great crime, but it carried a laid-down penalty of six months' jail.

'He is guilty,' said the Rabbi. 'He received stolen goods. The officer coming next week won't want to hear about our shortage of flour or how Yeltov helped the whole town. He is guilty of a crime, and –'

'He is the town's *only* baker,' said Klapyov flatly. Mark paused. It was true. He had forgotten. The matter was then doubly serious. And without solution as far as he could see.

'We have a solution,' said Klapyov. 'We have only one baker but we have also Pitzik the Pauper, who sleeps rough and is never sure where his next meal is coming from. He is not very bright, has no family at all, is no trouble to anyone – and looks a bit like Yeltov. The examining officer is not coming to examine anything really, or to look at anything – or anybody – closely.'

'You mean,' said Mark, 'that Pitzik should take the place of –'

'Yes. It is practical and sensible. For six months Pitzik will have a roof over his head and regular meals. He will have visitors from the town whenever permitted, who will take him gifts of food, etcetera, in gratitude. He will return to us a hero.'

'Gratitude?' said Mark.

'Gratitude,' said Klapyov firmly. 'For the town must have bread. And it will, because of Pitzik, who already feels proud of the new place in the community which will await him. In our opinion, Rabbi, and we have lived longer than you, the baker committed no crime and deserves no punishment.'

'Does Pitzik deserve punishment?' asked Mark, still troubled.

'Punishment? What punishment? Such a life for half a year will be for Pitzik a *punishment*? Come, Rabbi, what do you not understand? Am I to say it all again?'

'No,' said Mark. 'I understood every word. Thank you.'

22

The Rabbi was in a pensive mood. The day was mild and the synagogue was quiet. The service was over and he was alone. He loved his little synagogue, which needed a bit of paint and had been his domain for a long time. As a young man he'd come to this little town, with its odd people and its market-place, and here he'd met Sophie and here he'd stayed. The terrible cruelties of the Czar had with God's help passed them by and things could have been worse.

His eye fell upon the book open on his knee on the words said so often in the service, the prayer for the Return said by all Jews: 'Next year in Jerusalem.'

The Rabbi, who had his own humour, would have snorted in disbelief if some fool had told him stories about Jewish soldiers who would one day win wars in six days and fly half-way down a great continent to rescue a hundred of their brothers and sisters from a black madman at Entebbe.

The Rabbi knew nothing of flying. It had yet to come. And Jews were not soldiers unless they had to be by order of the Czar. There were commandments about how you treated others. The Rabbi smiled as a famous story came into his mind about the pale young Talmudic scholars torn from their books and thrown into the army by the Czar. To everyone's surprise the young men became great marksmen, with quiet eyes and steady hands, who notched up incredible scores at the target ranges. Then they were sent to the front line and when the enemy attacked the officer shouted, 'Fire!' And again, 'Fire!' And the young men looked at him, puzzled. 'Fire!' he screamed. 'Why don't you fire?'

'But there are people out there,' the young men replied. 'Someone could get hurt.'

The Rabbi sat on. To be a Jew was hard but it had always been so. Chosen people perhaps, but chosen for what? Mind you, considered the Rabbi, who knew his Bible, we certainly deserved some of the things God did to us. Disobedient ungrateful lot, needing miracles all the time. No wonder God is merciful and endlessly patient. He needs to be.

The Rabbi, who had a fine imagination, could not have taken in the fact of the Holocaust and the six million dead, many of whom would be the descendants of his little flock. The Cossacks and the Czar's police were the storm-troopers of his time but the bitter-sweet gallows humour of the Jews was the same. The Rabbi's own humour

came from his gentle father, who was one day
confronted by an enormous Cossack officer, very
drunk, who held him up to eye-level.

'The whole blasted world is in a mess!' roared
the officer. 'Agreed?'

'Agreed,' said the Rabbi's father.

'And it's all the fault of the Jews. Agreed?'

'And the bicycle riders,' said the Rabbi's
father, and the officer put him down.

'Why the bicycle riders?' said the officer.

'Why the Jews?' said the Rabbi's father, and walked away, to live another day.

The Rabbi sat on, a sermon forming in his mind, about respect for the lives of others and about leavening each day with humour and about the dream of the Return to the Land. Next year, dear Lord, with your help, in Jerusalem.

23

The morning service was over and the Rabbi was in his little office over the synagogue and feeling very peaceful. The Spring had positively begun and the sun was shining, and the air had a mild gentle feel about it. He'd enjoyed his walk to the synagogue in the early part of the day when few people were about. An ordinary weekday; no Sabbath, no feast or fast. Spring, peaceful.

Mark felt good, and put water on to boil. A glass of tea before anything else. He heard the downstairs door open and close, and a voice.

'Are you in, Rabbi? Are you receiving visitors? Is it a bother? A nuisance?'

It was Isaac the Beggar.

'Come on up,' called Mark. He was pleased, for Isaac was good company and in no way a bother or a nuisance, unlike some of the towns-folk of Klaneshtetl, who demanded rather than requested, who wanted miracles, and right away.

From Mark the beggar never wanted anything. A thing of mutual respect, and a similar kind of humour too.

Isaac settled himself, at home and relaxed, as he was wherever he found himself. 'I know your tea-making time, Rabbi,' he said, 'it saves me going home to make my own. Mind you, you're always welcome at my place. Any time, day or night.'

'I don't know where you live,' said Mark. 'Often I don't see you for weeks. Odd. It's never occurred to me that you live here in Klaneshtetl.'

'I don't,' said the beggar. 'Well, not all the time, anyway.' He smiled. 'I live here and there, in different kinds of establishments, some of which I wouldn't invite you to, Rabbi.'

'Odd,' said Mark again. 'After all this time I don't even know if you are married, let alone where you live. And I'm a sort of nosey feller.' Then Mark remembered that Isaac had a great skill in turning a question, in changing the subject. A private man. 'It's how you want it, isn't it?' said Mark.

'Well,' said Isaac, 'it doesn't do for everybody to know my business. It's better that I know everybody else's business. How else can I be their conscience?'

Mark chuckled. It was true. Isaac was a fearless critic of affectation and hypocrisy. There were many stories.

'I'm not married,' said Isaac. 'I nearly was once.' He took his tea. 'Thank you, Rabbi. A nice woman. A widow, very respectable. Very fond of me, but wanted to change my way of life. No more begging, no more buy and sell, no more live-by-wits. She had some fancy plans for me. I offered a deal. Come share my life for a year, I told her, then we'll get married, and you can make me respectable. She wouldn't hear of it. But I wouldn't budge and she liked me. So in the end she agreed and we went where no one knew either of us.'

'What happened?' asked Mark.

'At the end of the year she was the real thing. Every trick in the book. Better than me. She'd found herself. A born beggar-woman. Happy the whole day long. She and I parted on the best of terms, without a backward glance. I was delighted. After all,' said Isaac, sipping delicately, 'if I'd wanted to marry a beggar-woman I could have done so anytime.'

24

It was a fine cold morning and the snow sparkled. The Rabbi was enjoying the ride. It was not often he rode in such a fine carriage with a prancing white horse and a liveried coachman. Very grand. Mark smiled to himself. The poor Rabbi of Klaneshtetl sent for by the richest man in the province to help with a problem. A family problem. The rich man and Mark had been at school together and had kept in touch over the years. Less so of late, so the message to Mark had been the more surprising. 'A family problem,' said the note, 'please come. I'll send my carriage for you. More when I see you. Regards to Sophie. Reuben.'

Mark sat, warm in a large fur blanket, admiring the smooth movement of the white horse. The miles went past, then off the road through high gates and the seemingly endless tree-lined avenue up to the great house. Mark was impressed. His connection with his old school-friend had not been of a visiting kind.

He was warmly welcomed by Reuben, who was heavily built and richly dressed. Mark was shown to a fine room, to rest. 'We'll talk later,' said Reuben. 'And you'll meet the family.'

Mark sensed that the 'talk' was best done as soon as possible, without family.

'Give me half an hour,' he said, 'and come up. I'm not so tired.'

Reuben looked grateful and left it no longer. He was preceded by a footman, with drinks and snacks. When the servant had gone the two men relaxed; brought each other up to date.

'It's my son,' said Reuben at last. 'My only son. He has a bad attack of religion. Don't smile, Mark. We are not very orthodox Jews in this house, but we do observe, and my daughters and my wife are careful and we enjoy our religion. But even if we were ultra *ultra* orthodox it wouldn't suit my son. There's not an observance or fast or prayer he doesn't know about and perform. Nineteen years old. Perfectly normal until about six years ago. It gets worse and worse. It's serious, Mark.'

Mark knew it was. He'd had some experience of the wild-eyed zealot, the over-the-top fanatic, the religious *addict*.

'What does he want, your son,' he asked Reuben. 'To be a Rabbi?'

'I think,' said Reuben, 'that he wants to be a saint.'

The young man did not join the family for

dinner. He was fasting and praying, the footman said. Mark met him the next morning. He came to Mark's pleasant room which looked down on the stable yard covered in snow. The young man was articulate and learned. Widely read. He treated Mark with a certain condescension which the Rabbi ignored. Mark was looking behind the priggishness for a gleam of humour, of tolerance. It did not seem to be there, and Mark was sad, but last night's meal had shown a rich vein of laughter in the family. He interrupted the boy's rather opinionated flow.

'You dress like an Elder of the old times,' said Mark.

'Yes,' said the young man. 'Always in white. I dress only in white.' He carefully listed his pieties. 'I drink only water. And I mortify myself. I lie naked in the snow, I have sharp nails in my shoes. Daily I have myself whipped on my bare back in penance.'

'Look down in the yard,' said Mark. 'The carriage horse, who is white from nose to tail, has just drunk water, which is his only drink, and is rolling now in the snow, naked. He wears shoes with sharp nails in and is whipped every day. Tell me,' said Mark to the young man, 'what are we looking at, a saint, or a horse?'

The boy drew breath to make a learned reply and then didn't, and smiled, and Mark felt hopeful.

25

In a small town like Klaneshtetl, the Rabbi, in those early-in-the century days, was more than just a minister. The townspeople paid his wages and gave him a house and wanted good value. So Rabbi Mark was everything, from psychiatrist to magistrate.

This was a magistrate day, in the little hall next to the synagogue. All fairly normal, except that Sophie was present, with two other wives. They were like Sophie. Sensible, caring women, inclined, as Mark would say, to take up the occasional cudgel. Indeed they were there today through a sense of injustice.

'It's a disgrace,' Sophie had said at breakfast. 'And must be put right. Because nothing ever goes right for poor Sam. He is a shlimazl, a man with no luck. He'd be better off a schlemiel. A fool can get lucky. Poor Sam. Covered in soup.'

Mark looked up. 'Soup? What soup?'

'Your own definition, my Rabbi,' said Sophie,

with mischief. 'The difference between a schlemiel and a shlimazl. A wedding. A waiter and a guest. The waiter upsets a full tureen over the guest. The waiter is a schlemiel, the guest . . .'

'Yes,' said Mark. 'Yes. Poor Sam. Covered in soup. True. Poor Sam. Let us go to court to judge the matter of poor Sam, for whom nothing goes right.'

It was true. The whole town called Sam 'poor Sam' or 'Sam the Shlimazl' and the matter to be heard in court was fairly typical in poor Sam's poor life. It would have passed, with Sam again the loser, but for Sophie, who'd taken up her well-used cudgel.

Mark sat in his big 'Judge's chair' patiently. It was nearly lunch-time and the morning's cases had been ordinary and dull. Now it was Sam's matter.

'Come forward, Sam,' said Mark, 'and tell us in your own words the whole thing.'

Sam was small and thin and poor and defeated. A shlimazl, head to toe.

'From the beginning, Rabbi?' he asked.

'From the beginning,' said Mark.

'In the street of the good shops, near the market,' began Sam, 'I found a leather money-bag with one hundred and fifty roubles in it. I couldn't believe it. I didn't know what to do. I couldn't sleep. The next day somebody read to me a notice on the synagogue board that Gulden the rich man had lost such a bag of money and would pay a reward to the finder. So I put on my other coat and took the bag to Mr Gulden. He counted the money, which I hadn't touched, and sent me away. No reward. Not a penny.'

'Thank you, Sam,' said Mark. 'Mr Gulden, please.'

Mr Gulden, with three chins and an astrakhan coat, didn't move, except to wave his ferrety-faced lawyer forward.

'My client,' said the lawyer, 'saw no reason to further reward the finder, who had obviously already rewarded himself amply.'

'Who, *Sam*?' said Mark. 'I beg your pardon, proceed.'

'My client counted the money, pointed out that there had been *two* hundred and fifty roubles in the bag and sent the finder away, deciding in his goodness of heart not to prosecute for theft.'

'Thank you,' said Mark, and met Sophie's eyes across the court. He took his time.

'Your client says there were two hundred and fifty roubles in the money-bag?' said Mark.

'Positively,' said the lawyer.

'Then positively,' said Mark, 'the bag found by Sam cannot be your client's. It contained only one hundred and fifty. Bag and money to be returned to finder. Next case after lunch.'

26

The Rabbi had been looking forward to his trip for weeks. An old friend was going to stand in for him and live in his house and Sophie would look after him, and the Rabbi was free.

'Off you go, Mark,' said Sophie, 'go and see your old teacher. Go and look at pictures, and to the opera. Moscow has those things.' And she had given him a little money and seen him off.

Moscow was magical. The lights, and the glitter of the Czar's soldiers who seemed to be everywhere. The sharp contrasts of great wealth and absolute poverty, the marvellous art galleries, the sumptuous opera. And the quiet times with his old teacher, in whose small house he stayed. On the last night of his short holiday the old man was in his best, most gentle mood. He, Joseph of Dubno, one of the greatest preachers of his time, and Mark, one of his favourite pupils, had been discussing parables – more used, it seemed to

Mark, in the New Testament than in the Old. And not much used by Mark at any time. He was a bit blunt, was Rabbi Mark, with a hard truthfulness in him too much for some people; and the old man knew it. He took a pinch of snuff and looked over his spectacles at Mark.

'Here is a parable about Parable,' he said, 'who was one of twins, his brother being Truth. When young they looked alike but as they grew they became less alike and went different ways. Parable was the better observer of men and more amenable to change. Truth, when young, went always naked and people did not mind. To see a little naked Truth did no-one any great harm. But when Truth grew up and became man-size and still went naked his life was hard and people kept away from him. They were shocked and frightened by naked Truth and wouldn't have him in their homes and protected their children from him. And thus it was.

'One day Parable came along. He was a sight to see. From head to foot he was a joy to behold. Of many colours were his clothes and his hat was finest silk. His shoes were of the softest leather and he approached without noise. "What is this, brother?" he said, "so sad, so long-faced, naked and cold."

'Truth told him, truthfully, of his sad life. "Everybody avoids me," he said. "I have no place anywhere. I am old and finished."

' "Rubbish!" replied Parable. "We are the same age. And I am welcome everywhere. People

don't mind me one bit. You see, brother, people are funny. They don't like things naked and straightforward. They like things fancied up and a bit false, like me. Come, we are still the same size, we are twins. I will give you some of my finery. I've got lots, and it will change your life."

'And it did,' said the old preacher. 'Soon the twins were inseparable. You could hardly tell them apart. And Truth, dressed like Parable, was welcome everywhere.'

Mark went home the next morning and for some days seemed very thoughtful, thought Sophie, who had far too much sense to remark upon it.

27

It was nearly the end of the evening service and the Rabbi's mind was wandering a little. It often did at this time. After all, he knew the words, it was an ordinary Wednesday, neither fast nor feast, and the quiet murmur of the small congregation did nothing to disturb his wandering thoughts.

An odd day it had been. The first thing had been the new trousers for the coming High Holy Days. Knowing how long Schneider took to make anything, he'd allowed lots of time. The tailor was a marvellous craftsman but would not hurry for anyone – an absolute perfectionist. Six weeks he'd taken. One pair of trousers. Delivered that morning, tried on and pronounced perfect by Sophie – who had a good eye. 'Mark, they are beautiful,' she said. 'You are the most elegant Rabbi in Russia.'

Schneider had chuckled, and accepted his payment with dignity and stayed for a glass of tea. 'Tell me,' Mark asked him. 'If God managed to make the whole world in six days how comes it takes you six weeks to make one pair of trousers?'

The tailor pondered. 'Look first at the world,' he said, 'then look at your trousers.'

And then there there'd been the rich man from Moscow in his own coach with a matched pair of greys and a liveried coachman, who'd come back to his home town of Klaneshtetl to see his old mother and to visit the Rabbi also, and leave a generous donation for the old people's home. In gold.

Mark thanked him and the man waited, one eyebrow up, quizzically. 'The last time we met,' he said, '*you* gave *me* money.' Mark was puzzled. 'I don't remember that,' he said, 'but I'm sure we have met before. . . .'

'It's a fair time ago,' said the man. 'You were new here and I'd just got out of the Czar's army, curse him. There was no work anywhere round these parts so I went to Lublin and heard of a government job – as a public toilet keeper, and I brought the application form back for you to fill in for me because I couldn't read or write. And you told me the form said that to be a toilet keeper in Lublin you had to be able to read and write and that was that.'

'I remember,' said Mark gently. 'What then?'

'Then you gave me a little money and I bought shoe laces and matches and went back to Lublin, to the market. And made a few kopeks on the laces and bought more, and ate once a day only and saved and bought a stall, then two, then two more. Then a shop, then a bigger one, then two, then ten, then twenty. Then into land, and building, and this and that. Thank you for the start.'

Mark laughed. 'You're welcome,' he said. 'You've been busy. Did you ever find time to learn how to read and write?'

'No,' said the man. 'And I know what you are going to say. With all you've managed to achieve, you are going to say, just think what you might have been today if you'd been able to read and write.' And the man began to laugh and so did Mark and when Sophie came in they told her and they all laughed till they cried.

28

Mark was looking forward to his evening meal. Sophie had been busy on it all day, for a guest was coming. An old friend, from Sophie's youth, who was now the richest timber merchant in the region. His name was Joseph and he was a childless widower, a little bitter at the early death of his wife some two years before, but a pleasant kindly man who did good in his own way. The best way. By stealth. He visited rarely, for he lived a fair way away, but this was something of a special occasion.

'I started the whole thing,' Sophie said as Mark helped her lay the table, 'and it's only right that Joseph should get the best meal I can do. He deserves it. Not because he is used to a fine table – although I don't think so since poor Tanya died – but because he joined in and made a dream come true for someone.'

Mark chuckled. His Sophie was a marvellous mixture of rock-solid common sense and uncrushable romanticism.

Joseph came in his own carriage, with flowers for Sophie and a rare book for Mark. 'And a little wine for the table – and you must not argue, my Sophie, for am I not if not an Angel of the Lord at least on the staff?'

The meal was splendid, with Sophie toasted often, for her cooking, her goodness, her imagination – and her chutzpah. 'The most refined form of chutzpah,' said Joseph. 'To send me a special delivery letter which interrupted a board meeting and which was not really addressed to me at all! Mind you, I'm not complaining.'

'I should think *not*,' said Sophie. 'I wouldn't pass on such a letter to just anybody.'

Mark encouraged Sophie to retell and enjoy again the whole story. Her eyes glowed and her voice was warm and full of laughter. It was such a good story.

It had begun about two months before. Sophie had visited an old very poor couple on the edge of the town. As always she took food with her. The old people, a little shaky and vague, had welcomed her and told her all their news, mostly about their only granddaughter who lived far off with parents equally poor and struggling who certainly could not afford the wedding and dowry that their daughter richly deserved.

'So I've written a letter to God,' said the old man, whose name was Salman. 'We have no-one else to ask for help. Two hundred and twenty-five roubles will pay for everything. It's a lot of money but when God reads the letter he will understand.'

'Where did you send the letter?' said Sophie.

'The wind comes from Heaven,' said Salman. 'So it must go back to Heaven.' (His old wife had nodded in happy agreement.) 'So we put the letter on the little stone wall on the top of the windy hill. The wind will take the letter. A hard climb for us, but it's the best place.'

It was a fairly hard climb for Sophie too, when she took her leave. The letter had fallen down behind the wall. Sophie clambered over, recovered it and took it home. The shaky handwriting and perfect faith made her weep. The next morning she sent the letter with one of her own to Joseph, special delivery.

'And you replied on paper headed Department of Ways and Means, Heaven,' said Sophie, 'saying that the matter would be attended to with all dispatch and signing it "yours celestially".'

Four days later Joseph had gone, unknown to Sophie, to the old couple. He'd explained carefully that he was regional agent for the Almighty and one of his duties was to provide funds where needed to deserving cases to pay for modest weddings, including a small dowry. The figure arrived at in this particular case was two hundred and twenty-five roubles 'which is in this little velvet bag and no receipt will be required and will you wish the young couple good luck from my colleagues and myself.'

'To go *yourself*,' Sophie said lovingly. 'In a carriage with two white horses. Wearing a white fur hat!'

'Both hat and horses were to hand,' said Joseph modestly. 'It seemed correct procedure at the time.' He went on to tell again of the old couple's dignity, their lack of *surprise* at his visit. Deep gratitude, expressed with tears and laughter, not to *him* but to be conveyed *by* him to God when he got back to Head Office. His own position, as money-bearing messenger rather than benefactor, was shown him with perfect manners.

'A sort of lesson,' Joseph said to Mark. 'I think it shows that when the Talmud says that it is best that the giver of alms should be unknown to the receiver it could mean that the giver is entitled to be protected from the receiver.'

'Why do you try to be a cynic?' said Sophie happily. 'You with the white hat.' But Mark, who knew Joseph very well indeed, said nothing, until later, when Sophie was out in the kitchen.

'When the old couple came back from the wedding,' he said, 'I visited them, to hear all about it. Just before I left them the old man told me that he thought the agent, you, had seemed too smart somehow, with a carriage and white horses and so on, and he wondered if perhaps God had given you more than two hundred and twenty-five roubles and you had kept some for yourself, as agents do.'

Joseph, wealthy and experienced man of business, chuckled, showing neither surprise nor annoyance.

'What did *you* say?' he asked Mark.

'I forbade them, in my most Rabbinic voice, to express such doubts again, to *anybody*, at any time. *Ever*!'

Joseph looked at Mark with great affection. 'Sophie deserves a fellow like you,' he said.

29

It was the late evening of a summer's day and the small bedroom was full of the red-gold light in the sky. The Rabbi sat by the bed and the old man in the bed was dying. He knew he was dying and he had no complaint. He and Mark were old friends. When the Rabbi had first come to the town they had found a great bond of humour. The old man, Mendel, had been in his time a great prankster, a practical joker of a kind very near to Mark's heart, for the Rabbi in his early days had been no mean hoaxer himself.

He sat quietly, sadly, but took comfort in the fact that Mendel had no pain. It was quiet in the room. He thought Mendel was asleep.

Mendel opened one eye.

'You remember when we first met, Rabbi? The lottery?'

Mark remembered well. Mendel had won a big prize in a lottery with a ticket number that he'd said he dreamt. A line of dancing sevens. Six of them. 'Six sevens! he'd shouted to Mark. 'Forty-nine!' Six sevens are forty-two, Mark had told him. Mendel had grinned in a way that the Rabbi was to know well.

'The prize was *fifteen thousand* roubles, Rabbi, he'd said. 'Are you *sure* what six sevens make?'

Mendel opened the other eye. 'You know what I said to the doctor when he told me what I had was terminal? Terminal, Sherminal, I told him, as long as I have my health and strength!'

Mark chuckled. He had heard. The doctor, a man without humour, had been shocked.

'You know Rabbi,' said Mendel, my grand-daughter's husband has no knowledge of either drink or gambing.'

'That's a good thing,' said Mark gently.

'No,' said Mendel. 'It's bad. For he likes to do both. You know, Rabbi, when you are like me, you have deep thoughts, and I think, Rabbi, that life is like a glass of lemon tea.' And Mendel closed his eyes.

Mark pondered. Indeed a deep thought for Mendel. 'You want to tell me why?' he asked.

There was a long pause. Then the same wicked eye opened.

'How should *I* know?' said Mendel. 'What am I, a philosopher? My wife, God rest her dear soul, could never get over the fact I couldn't read or write. She could, and she was a great help to me in the shop. All important pieces of paper I would sign with an X. Do you know, Rabbi' (again the wicked look), 'when we opened our second store and moved to a bigger house she made me sign with *two* Xs?'

The old man was near the end. Mark had sat by many deathbeds, often of people he'd known a long time, but this was a special friend, this Mendel. This Mendel, who sensed the Rabbi's grief and made jokes.

Old Mendel's breathing grew shallow but he was not quite done. His look at Mark was innocent now, and loving.

'One last wish, Rabbi,' he said, his voice rather faint.

'Anything, old friend,' said Mark, bending forward to hear the words.

'When it's all over,' said Mendel, 'and it's time to lift me into my coffin, promise not to hold me under my arms ... I'm ticklish.'

30

One day just after Mark and Sophie had finished supper they had an unexpected visitor. But no less welcome, because they liked him. Isaac, the Town Beggar, though beggar was the wrong word really. 'This little town of Klaneshtetl needs me,' Isaac would say. 'I am its conscience, a warning to others. I know everybody, *well* – and well they know it!'

Sophie made him come to the table and fed him. He was at ease, as always, full of gossip – which Sophie loved, being no gossip herself.

At last Isaac leant back. 'Rabbi,' he said to Mark, 'I have a donation for you to help with the new schoolhouse next to the synagogue.' And he put a heavy bag of coins on the table.

Mark blinked. 'From you, Isaac?' he said.

'From Blindl the Miser,' replied Isaac calmly.

'Blindl the Miser!' exclaimed Mark. 'You're joking.'

'He's never given a penny to anything,' said

Sophie. 'Beastly old man, full of greed.'

'Five hundred roubles,' said Isaac.

Mark was flabbergasted. God is good. 'You mean Blindl gave you five hundred roubles to bring to me?'

'Er – not exactly,' said Isaac. 'What he gave me I sold for five hundred roubles.' And he would say no more.

When he had gone Mark and Sophie sat up a bit composing a fine letter to Blindl, for the gift was magnificent.

It was never delivered. By mid-morning the next day all hell had broken loose. The town was buzzing. A demand from old Blindl the Miser that Mark should immediately convene a Rabbinical Court for Isaac the Beggar to be charged with theft of an article of great value. The old miser was screeching and made no mention of donations or schoolhouses. But he was within his rights and Mark got on with it, rather worried for Isaac – and for himself, for he was an accessory, sort of. Good cause or not.

The courtroom was packed. Old Blindl, who had no teeth and a screeching voice full of anger, was so hard to understand that Mark asked Isaac to tell the truth and nothing but the truth, telling Blindl to listen to every word.

Isaac smiled at the Rabbi and began. 'I called on Mr Blindl for money towards the schoolhouse. His servant threw me out. When I reached home I found one of Blindl's big silver spoons in my pocket. The next day I returned it to him

with one more, smaller, which the larger one had given birth to overnight. He was interested and when I asked to borrow a large silver goblet he gave it willingly.'

The Court laughed and Mark, straight-faced, shut them up. 'Proceed,' he said.

'The next day,' continued Isaac, with a face

as straight, 'I took back the goblet with its child and Mr Blindl was happy to give it a home. He then asked me whether a gold watch set with diamonds could have young. I said I did not know. He gave me the watch to see if it was fertile. The next day I went back and told Mr Blindl that the watch sadly had died and I had arranged the disposal of the remains.'

The Court was in uproar. The laughter could be heard across the square. Mark hammered for silence. Now only old Blindl's screech could be heard. 'A judgment!' he yelled. 'A judgment! How can a watch die?'

'Blindl,' said Mark sternly. 'Be silent. And hear a question. If you accept that a spoon can bear a spoon and a goblet can give birth to a goblet, how can you stand before us and say you do not believe that a watch can die?'

31

In a small town like Klaneshtetl everyone knows everyone else pretty well, and, not as good, everyone knows everyone else's business. This story is about business, and Rabbi Mark and Sophie, whom we know, and three men of business whom we don't know, and will not meet again. Three rather dazed men of business, at the end.

But first, the horse. It was old and slow and lived in the field next door to Mark and Sophie's house and Sophie and the horse were friends. Sophie, who had time for everybody, also made time to feed and talk to the horse. Mark would make jokes about his four-legged rival with the sad eyes next door. 'I feed him and my wife keeps company with him and what does he do for me? Nothing.'

One day when the Rabbi went home from the synagogue after the morning service Sophie gave him a note signed by three men asking him to give a Rabbinic judgment on a business matter of some complexity and would it be all right if they called that evening. They were all from the other end of the town and their names were unfamiliar to Mark.

'Three-times-a-year-worshippers,' said Sophie. 'How would you know them? You can't know everybody.'

'A complex business matter?' said Mark. 'I don't think I'm their man. Stay in the room, Sophie, when they come.'

The men were different in appearance but all had the same worried look. They did not seem to like each other too much. One spoke for all three.

'We formed a partnership,' he said, 'to start a business to deal in horses. We put together twenty-seven hundred roubles. I put up half, he put up a third and he put up a ninth.'

Mark blinked. 'Er – yes?' he said.

'We bought seventeen horses,' said the man. 'Now we want to wind up the business. He doesn't like *him* and I can't get on with *him*. This is not a good time to sell horses and lose money so we want to share out the horses. But we can't. There's no such thing as a half of seventeen horses, or a third or a ninth. Give us a judgment, Rabbi.'

Mark was absolutely stumped.

'The Rabbi,' said Sophie, 'will deliberate upon this matter overnight and give you an answer tomorrow morning at eleven. Return then, bringing the horses.'

She showed the men out and came back, her eyes twinkling. 'Take it off your mind,' she said to Mark. 'I have a friend who will solve this problem for you. Come, to bed.'

The next morning as the time approached for the men and horses to arrive, Mark said: 'Sophie, how will your friend know he is needed? Should you not send a message?'

'He's here,' said Sophie. 'In the field. The eighteenth horse.' Mark stared, and then laughed till he cried. Then he put on a straight face and when the men arrived he put Sophie's friend with theirs. 'Eighteen horses,' he said. 'Half for you: nine. A third for you: six. A ninth for you: two. Now I must put the horse back in the field. Good day.'

He and Sophie watched the procession leave. He kissed her. 'I still don't understand,' he said.

'How could you?' she said. 'You are a Rabbi. How could you know about horses?'

32

Mark looked around the synagogue as he neared the end of the service. There was a suppressed feeling of excitement in the air – and many more people than usual on an ordinary Sabbath. A maddening lot, the Rabbi thought for the thousandth time. He knew well why they were there. Not for his sermon. Not at all. No, today, after service, Schneider the Tailor was to say the words. In front of everybody.

Mark wasn't too put out. Or too worried either at the seeming humiliation of the little tailor, who had his own wit and strength. It was the latest happening in the long battle between the tailor and the butcher, Grobbek, of whom the tailor had once said, in a public place, 'It is only right that the butcher should look and sound like a bull.'

And it is only right, Mark thought, that the present disturbance should be ended here in synagogue, where it had begun, a month before.

The service on that occasion was for one of the minor festivals and both Grobbek and his enemy Schneider were present. The little tailor was overworked and poor and not often in synagogue. After the service Grobbek's voice was loud: 'Tailor! A job for you! I have some cloth for a suit! The tailor in Lodditch over the hill said I didn't have enough. If you can make me a suit out of it the job is yours. I won't pay a Lodditch price, but then you are not a Lodditch tailor!'

'Who sold you the cloth?' asked Schneider.

'Gimbel, in Polyntz.'

'I know him. He doesn't make mistakes. There will be enough. I'll make the suit.' Schneider left and Grobbek told everybody what a great favour he was doing the tailor.

Mark smiled to himself as he remembered the Sabbath service of last week and Grobbek's grand entrance in his new suit – with a new hat and gloves to finish it off. A splendid suit in every way for Schneider was an artist at his trade. After a moment or two Schneider came in, with his only grandson. A seven-year-old, in a new suit as elegant as the butcher's. Of the same cloth.

The laughter began and Grobbek nearly burst a blood vessel. Mark stopped it and conducted the service. After, there was a great row and sides taken and hard words like Swindler and Thief and Cheat. Schneider, who had been paid for the work, remained calm. When Grobbek had run out of breath he said calmly, 'The tailor in

Lodditch is no more nor less skilled than I. He told you the truth. There was *not* enough cloth for him. He has *two* grandsons.' The crowd enjoyed it. 'And,' continued the little tailor, gently, 'when I think of the price you beat me down to, the wrong one is being called thief here.'

That did it. Grobbek, who was rich, shouted of libel and defamation and slander and high courts and lawyers and prison. Mark took over, and by mid-week he announced that Schneider, on the next Sabbath, today, would make public announcement in synagogue. Grobbek, he would say, is not a thief. Those words. No more.

Now it was time. The crowd was silent. In front of the Ark, the tailor. He looked thoughtful and serious. 'Grobbek,' he said slowly, 'is *not* a thief?' And in wonder, 'Grobbek is not a *thief*?'

And he walked out, softly.

33

The Rabbi looked around the little hall with certain misgivings. He could see that certain pranksters were present and he knew why. It was the Government Inspector's visit which had brought them. This was his second visit and the little town's jokers had his measure. On his first visit they had left it to Mark to feel him out, to establish his type, for Klaneshtetl had experienced many Inspectors in its time, from ex-officer lechers to pallid bureaucrats. Jews, they were taught, being second-class citizens, are to be kept in their place, looked upon with suspicion, distrusted at *every* level, for they were *strange* people, with *secret ways*.

This new chap, Klaneshtetl had decided, could be handled. A familiar type. Not dangerous. Mark wasn't sure. Certainly there was great self-importance. A complete lack of humour. A sublime contempt for Jews and all things Jewish. Mark relaxed a little. The pranksters were not young, and knew to a hair how far they could go. The gentle baiting of officials was an ancient and honoured tradition.

Mark looked along the trestle table at which he sat. The Inspector was nearly ready, his look-alike aide by his side. They had put out their papers, pens, forms and blotters in identical fashion. As the Inspector folded his fingers in front of him so did his assistant. The Inspector's eyes were cold, watchful, supercilious. His uniform was spotless, like his manicured hands. He was close-shaven, with short-cropped hair. He spoke:

'Report of insulting words and behaviour tenth of last month late evening outside Inn of Lodditch. Name: Glitchik, Boris. Step forward.'

From the aide, a thinner voice: 'Glitchik, Boris. Step forward. Answer all questions without lies. Make no statements.'

Glitchik was a fat man who worked with cows but hated milk. 'Not my kind of drink at all,' he was inclined to say. Indeed not. Nearly every other kind of drink was, though. A very happy drunk, was Glitchik. At this moment, sober, his bright eyes showing more mischief than guilt.

'Lewd gestures,' read out the Inspector. 'And insulting words about our Beloved Czar. Swindler. Thief. Glutton. Drunkard. Lecher. Half-wit. Do you deny using those words?'

'No, your Excellency,' said Glitchik. 'But –'

'Such words about the Czar constitute sedition and treason of the most –'

'– but not about the Czar, your Honour.'

'– serious and . . . what did you say?'

'Not about the *Czar*! The Beloved *Czar*! No, about the *Kaiser* who *hates* Jews and has informers all over *his* country listening to poor people. A mistake, your Highness. I swear it.'

'You swear it?'

'Of course. Such a mistake can easily happen if those words are used. . . .'

Mark was motionless, like everybody in the room. This was the thinnest ice, a most dangerous opening. The Inspector's eyes searched Glitchik's face, which was innocent and apologetic.

'I see,' said the Inspector. 'Very well. Be more careful another time. Next.'

'Application for a residence permit,' said the aide. 'To live in St Petersburg. Reason given: Specialized and essential trade. Volitch, Yossel.'

Mark hid his face behind his hand. This Yossel was a true joker, of original and inventive mind. A butcher and slaughterman. What specialized and essential trade?

'What specialized and essential trade?' asked the Inspector coldly.

'I am an ink-maker,' said Yossel. 'A maker of inks. Essential in a fine place like St Petersburg, your Splendidness, where writing and reading takes place to every side, day and night, and –'

'What's specialized about making ink?' said the Inspector nastily. 'Any fool can make ink. *I* could make ink!'

'And you *should*!' said Yossel staunchly. 'Then

130

perhaps *you* could apply for permission to live in St Petersburg!' As the Inspector went purple, 'Application refused, your Elegance?'

'Positively,' said his Elegance, feeling he'd been hit from behind in some way. 'Just a moment.' He looked at papers, importantly. 'What else do you do?'

Yossel paused, glancing at the Rabbi, who frowned warningly.

'I am a minyan-man.'

'A what?'

'A minyan-man.'

'Explain.'

'When there are nine persons in the synagogue waiting for a tenth so that prayer can begin I join them and that makes ten.'

'What new rubbish is this?' rapped the Inspector. 'If *any*body joins himself to nine it makes ten. If *I* join nine, it makes ten!'

Yossel beamed. Then to the crowd, in a voice full of joy: 'Our new Inspector is JEWISH!'

There was uproar. Screams of laughter, bangings of gavels, shouts for silence from the uniformed ones – and from Mark – whose ribs were aching. The crowd knew the game. They milled about, pushing papers off the table, jostling, pushing, getting Yossel out and away. The Inspector and his aide tidied their bits and pieces, called a recess, smoothed themselves down and moved with dignity towards the door. As they passed old Philber on the front bench they stopped. Philber sat forward, his left elbow on his knee and his chin in his hand. With his right hand he gestured and waved, his eyes on the floor, unfocused. His voice rose and fell, full of colour and argument. He answered himself, picking up points, outlining anew. It was fascinating to watch, the crowd was now silent, waiting. They had seen Philber do this before.

'I don't like to interrupt you,' said the Inspector at last, 'but do you realize you are talking to yourself?'

Philber stopped and raised sensible and unfriendly eyes. 'If you don't like to interrupt,' he said clearly, 'why do you? Do you realize I'm talking to myself, you ask. Tell me, your Eloquence, who else is worth talking to here?' He then began discussing the interruption with the floor.

The crowd parted and the Inspector and his aide left. Mark sighed happily. A nice start to the day. . . .

34

The Rabbi was a little worried. It was nothing new, the cause of his worry, but it had to be handled with care, for his flock was not as other people in small towns. They were more so; or less so. It depended a bit on what you were referring to. Less welcoming to strangers but more superstititious. Less provident but more generous on occasion. Less far-seeing but more complaining when their half-baked plans went wrong. Less trusting but more gullible when wild-talkers from big cities passed through.

And the latest wild-talker had come at the worst time. At the end of a very hard winter when the food was scarce and everyone was hungry and tired. There'd been illness and death and the little town was sad and its people stayed away from synagogue because prayer hadn't worked and it was all God's fault.

And suddenly there was the wild-talker with his mad eyes and white face and the waving hands and marvellous voice telling of the signs that the Messiah was due any time now. In days. A fortnight at the most. The Rabbi felt tired. He'd also had a hard winter. Sophie had been sick and so had he. And now this. He gave it careful thought. He sensed a waiting in the people, a superstitious looking for signs and omens. He made up his mind.

'A Special Meeting,' he posted up. 'To discuss the Coming of the Messiah. Thursday. After supper. In the Synagogue.'

The place was packed to the doors. He made them wait and then entered, with some majesty, in his full High Holy Days outfit. 'Very handsome,' Sophie said. 'Good luck, my love.'

He mounted the prayer platform and stood in front of the Ark till there was absolute silence.

'Who here,' he said, 'has not heard of Rabbi Joshua of Vilna?'

There was a storm of reply. 'Who has not heard of Joshua of Vilna? Is he mad? The wonder-worker of Vilna? Great Rabbi Joshua? The Jewel of God? The greatest Jew alive? The *world* knows him!'

'Good,' said Mark. 'Every year as a penance Rabbi Joshua used to dress as a beggar and wander for a month, far from Vilna, unrecognised, living on charity, going among people like us.'

'Has he been here?' the crowd shouted. 'Has he?'

'Who knows?' said Mark. 'Be quiet and listen, for we speak of a great man. At the end of one of these trips Rabbi Joshua was very tired and a long way from home. He sat by the road and along came a cart driven by a fat, dirty, drunken peasant. Joshua asked if he might get on. The driver agreed on condition that Joshua took the reins, and he rolled off the seat into the cart and went to sleep, snoring. And thus they came to Vilna and to Joshua's street. A man recognised him, then another and another and the shouts began, "The Messiah has come! The Messiah has come!" Other people rushed up. "Where? Where?"

' "Where?" shouted the men, "*Where*? If the Jewel of God, the Greatest Jew alive, Great Joshua himself is only the driver, who can be in the cart but the Messiah!" '

Mark waited. Then a young woman laughed, and another, then an old man, and soon the little synagogue rocked with great roars of joy. Mark relaxed. The winter was over.

35

The Rabbi walked home slowly. He had a little problem. Nothing very serious or requiring large gestures or strong action but nevertheless a problem. It had to do with how in a small town like Klaneshtetl there are few secrets and that tact and pride have always to be considered. A problem. And best talked over with his wife.

After they had eaten Sophie said, 'What is it, Mark?' for she knew her husband very well. 'You've been listening to me with only one ear.'

Mark chuckled. 'Forgive me, my love,' he said. 'A problem. Aaron the Cowman. You know him. His only daughter is to be married to a good young man as poor as Aaron is. She is a fine girl.'

'I know her too,' said Sophie. 'She *is*.'

'She deserves a little wedding,' said Mark, 'and Aaron is too proud to borrow money or to accept a loan – not that I know of anyone in this town who would lend money to a poor cowman.'

'Except perhaps you,' said Sophie. 'How much would it take?'

Mark hesitated. He was poorly paid and their savings didn't amount to much.

'Say forty roubles,' he said. 'Thirty-five maybe.'

'You think Aaron will ever pay it back?' asked Sophie.

'Positively,' replied Mark. 'First we have to get him to take it.'

'Alright,' said Sophie. 'Let's find a way.'

They stayed up late. The next day Mark went to see the cowman. Aaron was a big, simple man, rather surprised to find the Rabbi in his little house. After a few words about this and that Mark came to the point.

'When you go to Minsk,' he said, 'you can do me a favour.'

'To Minsk?' said Aaron. '*Me*, Rabbi? To *Minsk*?'

'You're *not* going to Minsk?' said Mark. 'I heard – perhaps I got it wrong – I thought – well, never mind. It's not urgent. No hurry. Funny, I thought you were –'

'What was the favour?' asked Aaron, 'perhaps –'

'No, no,' said Mark. 'I owe a man in Minsk forty roubles. I brought the money with me. No matter.' He turned away, turned back. 'Look, Aaron,' he said, 'who knows, perhaps for some reason or other, after the wedding you *will* find yourself in Minsk. Here, take the money. Anytime. The man isn't waiting for the money. Anytime. I'm obliged. Good. Er – if in the meantime you have need of the money, feel free to use it. You can replace it whenever it falls out that you *do* go to Minsk. Anytime. Here –'

Aaron took the money, troubled. 'Rabbi,' he said, 'I've never been even as far as Pinsk, let alone Minsk –'

'If,' said Mark, 'on the other hand I find that it is necessary for *me* to go to Minsk, which is very unlikely and has never happened yet, I will give you plenty of notice and I'll take the money back from you and deliver it myself. Good. I'm obliged. Give my regards to your wife and daughter. I look forward to the wedding.'

Aaron put out a big hand. 'Thank you, Rabbi,' he said.

'For what?' said Mark. 'For *what*? For doing me a favour? If thanks *were* necessary they should be to my dear wife Sophie who is good at getting money to people. Goodbye.'

36

The Rabbi was on his way back to Klaneshtetl and glad to be. The train seat was hard and the carriage was cold, but half the journey was over and in an hour or so he would be in his own house, with Sophie's good cooking and her loving interest in all the happenings of his two-day trip to Polyntz, a fair-sized city on the other side of the province.

As a rule there was little unusual to tell, thought Mark. These trips were generally for the same reasons. Synagogue business, or to fill in at a service for a sick colleague. Occasionally to preside at a wedding or funeral of moved-away-from-Klaneshtetl folk who would have no other than Rabbi Mark for such important matters.

Then Mark shifted and felt the big bruise on his backside. He smiled to himself. Yes, there *was* something to tell Sophie. Not about the first day or indeed the morning of the second day. All very ordinary and standard till then.

No, it had begun as he stood outside the rail-way station checking train times on the written-up notice. It was midday. Suddenly he received a great kick in the rump accompanied by a roar of laughter. Mark turned, in anger. He was middle-aged but strong and fit and ready to do battle. Facing him was a man of much his own age but bigger, his head forward, his hand outstretched.

'Boris!' he roared. 'Why, you old – Here, you're not Boris.'

'No,' said Mark. 'And there are other ways to greet a friend. My name is Mark.'

The man was crestfallen and embarrassed. 'Not Boris the Butcher?'

'No,' said Mark. 'Mark the Rabbi.'

'A *Rabbi*!' said the man. 'That's worse! I'm truly sorry, Reverend. Nothing personal, believe me, nothing anti-Jewish. I'm no Cossack, not militia or special police. A Rabbi! To kick a *Rabbi*!' He was truly contrite. 'I sincerely ask your pardon, Reverend.'

Mark's anger was long gone. 'Don't feel too badly,' he said, 'I'm less a Rabbi that end than this end.'

The man, after a moment, had chuckled.

'I didn't know Rabbis made jokes,' he said.

'Only after unprovoked bodily assault.'

The man pondered. 'How long before your train, Rabbi?'

'About an hour and a half.'

'Come and eat with me. I owe it to you. I don't often meet a Rabbi. Men of the cloth are

140

not my usual company. I sell guns.'

Mark was intrigued, and agreed. They went to a café not far from the station, where the man was obviously known. The owner was respectful in his greeting to 'Mister Litvinov' – who was asked to ignore the bill of fare and order whatever he liked 'and for your friend also'.

'Potatoes in butter and pork chops,' said Litvinov. 'Same for you, Reverend?'

'Some lemon tea only,' said Mark. 'There are certain restrictions as to what Jews may eat.'

'Of course!' said the gunseller. 'I know about it! Traif, right? Kosher is permitted, traif not. Right?'

'Right,' said Mark, and went into it a bit for his interested and lively new friend. When the food came it smelt and looked delicious. Mark strong-mindedly ate a boiled egg with his tea, watched with some amusement by Litvinov – who put away six pork chops in no time at all. As he wiped his moustache he said, 'They make up a marvellous seafood salad for me here. Lobster and crab with a sweet-sour sauce. Beautiful. Fancy, Rabbi?'

Mark shook his head.

'Traif?' asked Litvinov.

'Traif,' said Mark.

When the dish arrived it was beautiful, with a most delicate aroma.

'What,' asked the gunseller, 'if your very life depended upon eating traif? Do your Laws cover that?'

'Fully,' said Mark. 'Emergency Laws, where life – or even health – is endangered.'

Litvinov took a mouthful or two, looking at Mark with a set face. He put down his fork.

'This is some sort of Jewish joke!' he said suddenly. 'To pay me back for kicking you! A lot of blasted rubbish!' He kicked his chair violently away as he stood up. He opened his bag and took out a huge pistol. His eyes were murderous. He pushed his plate across to Mark. 'Eat!' he roared. '*Eat*! or I'll blow your blasted head off!'

Mark did as he was told, until the plate was empty. He wasn't too surprised when the gun was put back in the bag and the big man's smile came back.

'A boiled egg is no meal for a grown man,' said Litvinov. 'Don't be angry. A joke only. Say you are not angry, Reverend.'

Mark grinned. 'Why shouldn't I be angry?' he said. 'If you'd started your joke earlier I'd have tasted pork as well.'

They parted good friends, exchanging addresses. 'Come to us for a meal,' said Mark. 'Nothing traif, and the best cooking in the province.'

37

Sometimes, when the Rabbi had had a busy week, or a week more busy than usual, sometimes he had no time to prepare a Sabbath sermon. He would always manage, but it bothered him. His wife Sophie would say, 'Nonsense, some of your off-the-cuff talks have been marvellous!'

Mark would grin, for such ad-lib sermons would often have the sort of humour never far from the surface in his nature. Not all the congregation approved of humour in a Rabbi.

He looked at the congregation this Sabbath morning. There seemed to be more than the usual number of disapprovers in the not very large number of townsfolk. Odd how they vary, he thought. Sometimes, on an ordinary weekday, at the early morning service, just with the dozen or so worshippers, most of them old men, there was a real feeling of prayer; of a simple word with God. Not like today, thought Mark. Gabbled prayers, automatic responses, one eye on the clock. And no sermon prepared either. A busy week. Not an idea in my head. And a joke or two won't go with this lot. He felt a bit tired.

Suddenly there was a disturbance. The door was pushed back with a bang and a large ragged man staggered in. It was Mischa, the Town Drunkard. He stopped half-way down the aisle, looking round, surprised. The disapprovers glared and shushed and clicked their tongues. Mark waited.

'Oh, I'm sorry, Rabbi,' said Mischa. 'Got the day wrong. Thought it was a weekday. Go and have a lie down by the stove in the synagogue, I thought. The Rabbi won't mind. Sorry, Rabbi.'

'That's all right,' said Mark. 'You want to stay?'

Mischa looked round again. 'No thank you, Rabbi,' he said. 'Not with this lot. I'll come back when the place is empty and do me praying then.'

He lurched out and there was hubbub. A rather pious hubbub, thought Mark. It quietened and soon it was sermon time. Mark took his time before he began.

'Hear now a story of the Great Rabbi Avrom of Kovno, God rest his dear soul. He lived to a good age but did not enjoy good health. He was often ill. On one or two occasions very ill indeed, almost to death. The second time the whole town gathered for prayer to save the Rabbi. All shops were closed. The whole town. Everybody at prayer. Except the town drunkard, who went round banging on all the shop shutters trying to buy vodka. When it was explained to him why all the shops were closed he rushed to the synagogue and prayed also. "Almighty God," he shouted, "save our beloved Avrom – and *soon* – so I can get some vodka!"

'Avrom recovered. A near-miracle. And during the Passover a Thanksgiving Service was held and Avrom gave the sermon. He ended by thanking the people for their prayers. "You may think," said Avrom, "that God does not hear all prayers. But the drunkard's prayer he certainly heard, for it was from the heart!" '

Mark sat down. He looked up at Sophie in the women's gallery and she blew him a kiss.

38

The Rabbi was a little depressed. Not, he had to admit, with any good reason, and normally after the morning service on the Sabbath he felt good. He really enjoyed his few minutes by the synagogue door as the people left, his voice always warm as he wished them Shabbat Shalom, 'a peaceful Sabbath'. He solemnly shook hands with the children and was gentle with the old ones. A loving man, the Rabbi, with time for people. And he always enjoyed the walk home with Sophie and the good lunch and the Sabbath 'feel' of the house. And if there was an out-of-town stranger, someone passing through, even better. A guest! Talk of other places, bigger places, for indeed Klaneshtetl was small. Big enough, Sophie would say, bigger towns have the same people but more of them. Wise Sophie.

Today, a special guest, from a bigger place, standing by his side, bidding people a peaceful Sabbath, accepting their thanks for his marvellous sermon.

And his guest's sermon *had* been marvellous admitted the Rabbi to himself, for this was his old teacher, from Dubno, the Great Rabbi Joseph of Dubno, who stood smiling, with his wide white beard moving in the breeze.

The Rabbi, who was no mean preacher himself, had no jealousy of his old teacher, who had taught him all he knew. Then why, he thought, am I depressed? The sun shines, I am blessed in a hundred ways and my beloved teacher has honoured my synagogue with his presence.

On the walk home the old man chatted with Sophie, of whom he was fond. Indeed, he had officiated at her marriage to the Rabbi, Mark, his favourite pupil. A long time ago, now. Mark's rather silent walk did not go unnoticed. Neither did his quietness during lunch. After, when Sophie went up for a little rest, the old man tapped his finger on the table as of old.

'Speak,' he said. 'Clearly, using simple words.'

Mark, in middle age, felt like a student again. 'How do you make it fit so perfectly?' he said. 'We spoke for no more than twenty minutes before the service about a situation almost peculiar to this odd little town and you created in your sermon a perfect parable and lesson to point it up and show it truthfully. Twenty minutes!'

The old Rabbi waved a modest hand. 'Here is another perfect parable,' he said, 'to show your old teacher to you in more faithful colours – and

148

to cheer you up. A rich man sent his son to military academy to learn the art of musketry. For five years the young man learned the disciplines of perfect shooting. He graduated and left for his home, far away. The next day he stopped at an inn for a midday meal and to rest his horse. He ate outside and noticed on the nearby stable wall a number of chalk circles and in the dead centre of each was a bullet hole. He was amazed. What a marksman! He could not rest until he'd found out who it was. It was a poor boy, barefoot, who could not read or write and far too young to go to any academy.

' "How do you do it?" asked the graduate. "*How*?"

' "I shoot first and draw the circles after," said the boy.'

Mark chuckled, and waited. 'I do the same,' said his old teacher. 'I am blessed both with a good memory and a love of little stories, which I hear all the time. They are my chalk circles. Everywhere I go there are holes in walls, every one different. I find the right circle and draw it. Is there a little more wine?'

39

It was a matter that the Rabbi wished he had not to preside over, for his own feelings were involved, which was not good when he had to act as a judge in the monthly hearings. It was part of his work, but often provided great enjoyment and interest.

No, thought Mark as he settled himself in the shabby large chair that acted as Judge's throne, no, I do not like the Doctor of Polyntz and I *do* like old Bootzl (whose real name was Bitzel but who was called Bootzl because he was a cobbler).

Mark looked around. The little hall was fairly full, mainly of spectators, for this of Bootzl and the Doctor was widely known and sides had been taken, opinions offered. Some said how come a poor cobbler should go to the expensive Doctor of Polyntz, others said why not? If a wife like Leah – a woman above rubies – becomes very ill you go to *any*one, to the Almighty himself. Mind you, said others behind their hands or into their glasses, the Almighty might be cheaper.

And that, thought Mark to himself, is it, really. The doctor who charged high fees, knowing that among the poor towns in the region this could only mean he was a great healer, to be brought in or gone to when all home remedies had been tried, or the doctor who charged less had not been successful. Thus the Doctor of Polyntz had become very rich. He was no miracle-man. No better nor worse than any other well-trained experienced practitioner. Mark had met him on one or two occasions and had not been impressed. The man was full of long words and patronising tones. He was dressed and carriaged and housed *to* impress, to *look* expensive.

But Mark knew also that in the matter of collecting his fees, or 'value equivalent to', the Doctor was iron-hard, and had become part-owner of a number of businesses and farms in the province 'in lieu' of debts.

Bootzl sat quietly, to Mark's left. He looked what he was. A poor artisan, in his middle sixties, with the blackened powerful hands of his trade. He was pale, and sad, for his Leah had died. The costly Doctor of Polyntz had been powerless. His Leah was dead and he had no way of paying the Doctor's bill. Perhaps he should have asked at the beginning how much it was likely to come to.

Mark looked to his right. The Doctor, he noted, had no lawyer with him. He was very elegant and at ease, very used to this situation no doubt, thought Mark, doing his best to crush the uncharitable thought. He nodded to the Doctor and asked him to state his case.

The Doctor rose, putting his gloves and top hat next to his silver-topped stick on the seat beside him.

'I was brought in rather late in the lady's illness,' he said in a cultured, expensive voice. 'I promised I would do my best but made clear that there was not too much hope. I also made it quite clear that my fees were high.' He smiled thinly. 'As is fairly well known in this area. I was not asked what my fee would be. I paid in all three visits. I am owed a considerable sum and am given to understand that distraint and bailiffs may be necessary.'

'Thank you,' said Mark. 'Bootzl?'

The cobbler stood up, looking for words. Mark didn't rush him.

'I could sell the shop and my tools,' the grey little man said at last. 'There is some furniture. A brooch and gold ring of Leah's. The Sabbath candlesticks which are silver, which Leah lit every Friday night . . .' He stopped, his eyes down.

'First,' said Mark gently, 'tell us about bringing in the Doctor.'

'I was desperate,' said Bootzl. 'She wasn't getting better. Nothing did her any good. "The Doctor of Polyntz," somebody said. In fact more than one person. "He is famous, and has cured many. He costs a lot but who thinks of money at such times. The Doctor of Polyntz!" they said. "Famous!" '

Across from Bootzl the Doctor preened, looked around, stroked his silky beard.

'So I did it,' said Bootzl. 'He came and he was honest. Not much hope, he said, no certain cure, he said. No matter, I told him, no matter. Do your best. I will pay. If you cure her or kill her I will pay!' He went on till tears came and Mark stopped him. He looked at the Doctor, who showed in his face only distaste at such display.

'As no written contract exists,' said Mark levelly, 'we have to establish verbal contract. Agreed?'

'Agreed,' said the Doctor haughtily.

'In evidence we have heard that your late patient's husband promised to pay your fees whether you cured his wife or killed her.'

'Words to that effect, yes.'

'Words to that effect or those exact words? Exact words constitute contract.'

The Doctor looked at the Rabbi with a new respect.

'Those exact words,' he said. 'Whether I cured or killed her I would get paid. In full.'

Mark wrote it down carefully and slowly, and both Bootzl and the Doctor signed at the bottom. Poor Bootzl was beaten, his head down. The Doctor smiled at the crowd, who didn't smile back. Neither did they give off any warmth in Mark's direction.

'Now,' said Mark briskly as the Doctor was about to sit down again. 'The contract. Full payment whether you cured her or killed her. Did you cure her?'

The Doctor straightened, a frown beginning, some irritation too.

'You know I didn't. I explained –'

'Did you kill her?'

'Of course not!' snapped the Doctor and was going to be very cutting but then stopped, his eyes fixed on Mark's.

'If you didn't cure her and you didn't kill her,' said Mark, 'why do you expect payment? Why do you waste the time of this court? And of good Bootzl, who has shoes to mend?'

40

The Rabbi looked at his sleeping wife. No longer young, but in sleep her broad brow and firm jaw had a strength and peace that he found beautiful, as always. Mark was tired, it was late, he had stayed long in the houses of sick and bereaved people, but he sat with one shoe off and thanked God for his wife.

They were right, the old ones, he thought, when they said that in a community the Rabbi's wife, the Rebbitzen, was as important as the Rabbi. In some ways more important.

His own father, bless his memory, would tell a fine story against himself to show the value, above rubies, of a real Rebbitzen – in this case, *his* wife, for Mark's father had also been a Rabbi, a gentle spirit with no idea of how to obtain a post or sell himself.

'But your mother knew,' the old man would say to Mark. 'She knew how. "Stay among your books," she said to me, "leave it to me." And she did it. And when I was a young Rabbi, with my first flock, it went to my head and I became grand in my manner until one day your dear mother said to me: "You think I am the Rebbitzen because you are the Rabbi? You are the Rabbi because I am your Rebbitzen!" '

Now I have my own story against myself, thought Mark, his shoe in his hand, and he smiled, and I shall tell it as often, and with as much love, as the old man did.

Ten days before had seen the start of it. Mark, untypically, had made a play on words in his sermon, rather forgetting that in Klaneshtetl there would be people whose use of words was simple and their understanding of their Rabbi's words literal.

Mark had finished strongly, in ringing tones. 'God is just, and balances men, so that all are equal. Who is rich on earth will be poor in Heaven and he who is poor in this life will be rich in the next.' It had been much admired, his sermon. Even Sophie his wife had said a word or two, and made him glow. Six days later she had other words: 'A problem,' she said. 'Mindel, who keeps the corner shop and has no idea how to keep *any*thing, certainly not money, *and* is a gambler. He is in the parlour. See him now. I'll stay in the room. Don't argue, you brought it on yourself. He's been waiting two hours.'

As the Rabbi and Sophie went into the parlour Mindel got up. He talked at length with great conviction. 'Well, Rabbi,' he finished, 'there you are. I'm very poor indeed. So if you lend me a hundred roubles, in the next world I'll be rich and pay you back.'

The Rabbi, who didn't have much more than a hundred roubles in the world, felt he could not do other than stand by his clever words. He went to his desk for the money.

Sophie, blessed Rebbitzen, said, 'Mindel, what will you do with the money?'

'Buy new stock,' replied Mindel, 'paint the shop, make a success, sell the shop, buy two more, or a casino, or a racecourse, make a success, live in a big house –'

'– and you will be rich,' said Sophie. 'And so in the next life, poor. So how will you be able ever to pay back the money?'

The Rabbi took off his other shoe and bent over and gently kissed his Rebbitzen.

41

It was a serious matter; of that there could be no doubt. The Rabbi could not remember such a thing happening before, neither could he understand the Matchmaker, with his vast experience, getting himself into such a position. Motke's skill in the arranging of a marriage between young people who would meet for the first time on their wedding day was well known. Or if not on the Day only once or twice before the Day. It was the way of things. Parents knew best and Motke knew better than anyone. Many were the stable and perfect marriages begun in such a way.

And now here in the little room behind the synagogue was a young man, on the Day itself, with the families and friends of both sides already gathered, with the bride in the adjoining little room, *refusing* to go through with the ceremony! Determined to *not* get married to the lady in the next room. Not for *anything*, positively *not*. *No!*

Mark pondered, quite calm. It was not his way

to get excited. He did not know the young man very well. He knew the parents better. Ordinary people, who had put the matter of a bride for their son in Motke's hands in perfect confidence. Mark had heard that the son had lived in a city for a while and read modern books but had agreed to an arranged marriage to please his parents. Good, thought Mark, but he could see a certain young conceit in the wilful, rather weak face.

Motke also waited, as calm as Mark. Old friends, with respect for each other's judgment and subtleties. 'We sort of need each other,' the matchmaker would say.

'When I wanted to meet her, you said no,' said the flushed bridegroom. 'When I asked you questions about her you changed the subject. When you took me to her home to meet her parents she sat behind a screen. Well, now I know from my sister what she's like! You tricked me!'

Mark held up a mollifying hand and the boy quietened, looking round wildly, like a trapped animal. Mark could see that Motke was stern, with not a mollifying breath in his body. The Rabbi smiled inwardly. Experience tells. He waited for Motke to speak.

'Did I promise you a beauty?' said Motke. 'A city-lady? A heroine in a book?'

'She wears thick spectacles! She can hardly *see*!'

'So you lose her spectacles now and then and your life's your own.'

'My sister says she is so tongue-tied and shy she hardly speaks.'

'What, a wife should chatter all the time? Where is it written? Did I promise an entertainer, an actress, a speaker on subjects? The meal you ate at her parents' house *she* cooked. With few words but to please you. Next.'

The boy's resolution was weakening but there was fight left in him.

'You told me her father had been dead five years. He'd been *in prison* five years!'

'Not *dead*? To be in a Cossack prison is to be *alive*? Continue.'

'And all that business at the meal with silver cutlery and cut glass and stuff. Lace tablecloth! And *serviettes*! How do I know it was all *theirs*? Maybe they borrowed it all – to impress me!'

'Borrowed? Who do you think would lend to people like that?'

'And another th – what did you say?'

'I said you're not marrying the parents, you are marrying the daughter.'

'I'm *not*! She has one leg shorter than the other!'

'Build your house on a hillside.'

'Eh?'

'Where is it written that legs must be of equal length?'

'She *limps*!'

'Only when she walks. Next.'

The boy was near to tears. 'I'm too young to get married! I'm not ready.'

'What young?' said Motke, hard-faced, avoiding Mark's eye. 'What *ready*? Marriage is like measles. It comes to us all. To be married is good. What are we discussing here? A young woman who looks at everything closely, who does not chatter and waste words, who does not rush about dancing and playing outdoor and unfeminine games, who will work hard to keep you, whose parents do not owe because they cannot borrow. Who will make much of you and show their gratitude to the fine young husband of their only child.'

The young man turned desperately to Mark. 'Rabbi,' he said, his voice soft and urgent, aware of his bride in the next room, 'Rabbi, I beg of you —'

'You needn't whisper,' said Motke, 'She's a bit deaf. Come, Rabbi, let us begin.'

42

It has been shown before that Sophie was no fool, and even cleverer if her Mark was troubled by something. The trouble was at present in the parlour with Mark. The trouble was two men, brothers, who were dishonest and liars. They had made themselves rich and feared in the district and Mark was trying, as he did every year in the week before the Fast of Atonement, to make clear the meaning of the Fast, the chance to change, to repent, to stop such dishonesty and lying. Each year he would use the week to see the various 'bad ones' as Sophie called them. There were a number.

The brothers, who had the same cunning eyes, were quite unimpressed by the Rabbi, and indeed admitted nothing. Were rather hurt by Mark's straight talking. 'Where do you *get* these stories from, Rabbi?' they asked. 'All lies, put about by our competitors and enemies.' They could not be shaken.

Sophie pondered, and prayed. One of her direct little requests to the Almighty, who acted right away. A knock on the kitchen door. A stranger, with a strange favour to ask. Sophie listened and marched him straight through to the parlour. 'A traveller,' said Sophie. 'Passing through. He wants to fast and pray in our synagogue. He is carrying a large sum of money and wants to leave it in our care, Mark. I said yes, and that we will give him a written and witnessed receipt. These two gentlemen will act as witnesses.'

Mark, who knew Sophie's opinion of 'these two gentlemen', was a bit surprised, but Sophie had a certain look in her eye and he didn't argue. The money, in two leather bags, was counted and the receipt signed and witnessed. The man went off to the small inn on the edge of town. Soon after, the brothers left. Mark was rather low in spirit at his lack of influence with them. Sophie was cheerful and busy in her preparations for the important and – for Mark – exhausting day of fast and prayer.

On the morning after the fast was over, the stranger sent a message to say he would pick up his money-bags at noon. Sophie had a few words with Mark, who laughed out loud and kissed her warmly. Then she sent for the 'two gentlemen', who came, puzzled.

When the stranger arrived, Mark and the two brothers were waiting. Mark took the receipt back and locked it in a drawer.

'What money?' he said to the man. 'Money? I know nothing of your money. I've never seen you before in my life. These gentlemen were here in this room when you say you gave me this money and they will sign pieces of paper to say you were never here.'

The man nearly died of shock. He shouted, wept, nearly had a seizure, stuttered and was silent. The two brothers, licking their lips, calculating the share-out, signed the bits of paper prepared by fellow-villain Sophie.

Then Mark gave the man his money and Sophie took him into the kitchen to feed him and comfort him and explain to him.

Mark locked away the pieces of paper with the receipt. 'Let us,' he said to the brothers, 'discuss again the lies spread about you by competitors and enemies. Let us talk about atonement, the chance to change habits, the laws of written evidence, all sorts of things. And we will do it carefully and slowly . . .'

43

The Rabbi was spending a day or two with his old teacher and as always enjoying every moment. The old man was frail in body but of unimpaired mind and humour. A humour rather like Mark's own. This gentle wit of Rabbi Joseph of Dubno was widely known. Mark had been his favourite pupil. 'Not very clever,' the old man would recall, 'but hard-working and with a bit of fun in you, which I like in a young man. A Rabbi without humour is food without salt.'

Mark had been bringing his old friend up to date on happenings in Klaneshtetl. The old man was interested in everything. In particular he had listened when Mark told of a tendency lately in the little town, among certain of the better-off and more established people, towards a kind of holier-than-thou, pious attitude.

The evening before, over dinner, Rabbi Joseph and Mark had talked long about the Gospels.

Mark's old teacher, utterly devout in every way, was in no way narrow in his knowledge or teachings. His pupils were expected to know of both Testaments. He and Mark had discussed great moments. The cures, the great sermons, the trial. The old man had dwelt on the 'who shall cast the first stone?' question put by Jesus to the mob who were going to kill the adulteress. 'Great knowledge of people, the Carpenter,' Old Joseph had said.

Now he sat thoughtfully as Mark finished telling of another example of self-righteous behaviour in the town. Especially towards wrongdoers or people fallen on hard times.

'It's a pity,' said Mark, 'that I couldn't give them a good telling-off sermon using the "who shall cast the first stone" story as text. Wouldn't go down at all. I've tried using the Gospels once or twice. In a small Jewish town it is a mistake. Pity.'

Old Joseph smiled. 'The Carpenter didn't invent the parable,' he said. 'He used an existing teaching method. To a simple audience, simple terms. For farm people, farm images. For the sophisticated, words to suit. So here, Mark, is a little story, old and simple, like me.'

He settled himself. 'A man, very hungry, was caught stealing food from the King's storehouse and ordered to be hanged. He accepted the sentence but said he wanted to give to the King a magic secret of great value rather than have it die with him. The King was intrigued and went with his Court to the place of the gallows. The thief took a small bag from his belt. "These are magic pomegranate seeds," he said, and dug a small hole in the earth by his foot and then looked up. "If one seed is put in this hole by a man who has never in his life taken anything that didn't belong to him, the seed will grow overnight into a tree, bearing fruit. *I* cannot do it because I am a thief."

'The King took the little bag. "I also am not fit," he said, and went from one to another of his Court, every single one of whom drew back. Only the High Priest hesitated, and the King waited, but honesty is catching, and the High Priest also shook his head.

'The King went back to the thief. "You are free," he said. "For you showed us not magic but a mirror." '

44

The Rabbi would often say to Sophie that after twenty-five years in the same little town with all its odd people he could feel in the very air itself any disturbance, or change or trouble. 'Something in the air,' he would say. He was always right. Mind you, we are talking of simpler, less sophisticated times; sixty or seventy years ago, when superstition was a little nearer the skin in people.

'Something in the air,' he announced one morning.

'Again?' said Sophie across the breakfast table. 'What is it this time?'

'Odd questions in the synagogue and talk in the market about magic and impossible happenings and wonder-working Rabbis.'

'Ah,' snorted Sophie. She had her own opinion of so-called wonder-working Rabbis whom everyone had heard of and no-one had ever actually met. 'I tell you, Mark,' said Sophie, 'that if rumours were food this town would be fat. Are you worried about it?'

'Not really,' said Mark. 'Not really. But we've had this before, or similar, and the town gets a bit silly – and a bit dissastisfied with the Rabbi in this chair, who can't do magic *or* wonders. It needs thought.'

Mark left it for nearly two weeks and kept his ear well to the ground. He was not wrong. A whole buzz of rumour and hearsay was going on. He let it be known that his sermon on the coming Sabbath would be about wonders, and questions would be welcomed after service.

The synagogue was packed and Mark told the story of The Creation. Then of The Flood and then of The Plagues in Egypt and Moses. The congregation was not too impressed and if they took the point at all didn't show it.

The first one to ask a question was the butcher, Grobbek.

'Very nice, those old Bible stories, Rabbi,' he said. 'But what would you say about the wonder-working Rabbi of Plotsk who can turn himself into the Prophet Elijah every night?'

'What would I say?' said Mark. 'I would say it might not be true.'

'Not true!' shouted the butcher. 'Not true! Do you think that a Rabbi who can turn himself into Elijah every night needs to tell lies?'

The crowd roared its agreement and Mark felt he wasn't doing too well. There were more such questions. Mark thought he would try a little humour. It had worked before.

'This is a true story,' he said, and the crowd went quiet. 'Some years ago a wonder-working Rabbi came late at night to an inn. It was shut and the innkeeper refused, with much bad language, to open up and let the Rabbi in. It was a bitterly cold night. "Very well!" said the Rabbi. "At noon tomorrow this inn will burn down. I have spoken. Goodnight." The innkeeper, full of stupidity, was terrified, and rushed after the wonder-worker and implored him to accept the best of everything the inn had to offer. The wonder-worker ate and drank his fill and slept well, in the best room. He rose late and stayed long at breakfast, with the innkeeper eyeing the clock every minute. At half past eleven the wonder-worker got to his feet. "It has now been shown me," he said "that your inn will *not* burn down at noon today."

'And you know, my friends,' said Mark, 'it didn't.'

He expected a big laugh. Nothing. Then the butcher rose.

'Of course it didn't, Rabbi,' he said. 'The wonder-worker said it wouldn't.'

Mark felt he had a little way to go yet.

'Grobbek,' he said, 'you are a man of business. Your opinion, please, on another story. Of the wonder-worker of Odessa. To whom a cynic went one day, smartly dressed. The Rabbi gave him a pious greeting. "Thank you," said the cynic, and handed over ten roubles. "Thank

171

you," said the Rabbi. "A prayer for your barren wife?" "Not married," said the cynic, and gave another ten roubles. "Thank you," said the wonder-worker. "An intercession on your behalf for a sin? For an improvement in your health?" "I live clean," said the cynic. "Business is great, and I never felt better. Here's another thirty." "Thank you," said the wonder-worker. "What *do* you want?" "I want to see," said the cynic, "how long a man can sit there taking money for nothing." '

One or two people chuckled. Grobbek glared, and there was silence. 'The matter is simple,' said the butcher. 'Either the money should have been returned, or the customer given a credit note for a fifty-rouble miracle.'

A great roar of laughter went up, and Mark relaxed a little. There was hope yet.

45

'Sometimes,' said Sophie, 'sometimes this town gets me down. I don't know what gets into them. They make me sick.'

The Rabbi put down his book. He knew the feeling. His parishioners were, to say the least of it, a very odd lot. 'Tell me,' he said.

'I've just fed a beggar in the kitchen,' said Sophie. 'He has a hoarse voice and speaks roughly and is very ugly but there's no harm in him and he is strong and willing to work. He was starving, and has been in the town for three days! He's been insulted and turned away and treated like dirt!'

She went on a bit, getting pink in the face and upset until the Rabbi stopped her.

'Will you permit, my beloved Sophie,' he said, 'one of my little jokes?' She blinked away a tear but didn't reply because his face was unsmiling. 'Trust your Mark,' he said. 'And now take me to your ugly guest in the kitchen.'

The man *was* ugly, with a squint too, and a purple birthmark across his cheek to finish it off. One shoulder was higher than the other and his hands were huge. But Mark thought he could see humour deep in the crossed eyes and the big mouth and after a few minutes' talk he was sure. He spoke simply. 'Near the gate,' he said, 'is an icy patch. Slide on it, fall down with your leg under you and yell with pain at the top of your voice. Leave the rest to us.'

The man did as ordered and went down like a stone and bellowed like a bull.

'Good actor,' remarked Mark.

'Maybe he's really broken his leg,' said Sophie, worried.

Soon people came and the Rabbi and Sophie went out. Mark knelt. 'Fractured leg-bone and knee-joint,' he announced. 'Terrible pain. Four strong men to help bring him into the house, into the parlour, onto the couch. We will look after him. After all it was our icy patch by our gate.'

The small crowd watched as the man was installed. 'Anything we can do for the poor chap?' asked a woman who'd thrown slops over the poor chap the day before.

'No thank you,' said Sophie and shooed them out and closed the door.

Soon the whole town knew of the accident and people started to ask how the poor stranger was. 'Mending slowly,' Mark told them. 'A long job,' said Sophie.

Then people started to call, to bring good

things to eat, some fruit and nuts, a bottle of wine, some sweets, a picture-book, some cast-off clothing, some good boots. And when the Rabbi decided the poor invalid was well enough to move on a collection of money was taken up to help him on his way. He was given a friendly send-off by the town and as he and Mark shook hands the Rabbi said softly, 'Keep well, friend. Stay on your feet. Avoid slippery paths.'

The next Sabbath Mark offered a splendid sermon on the matter. 'How odd,' he said, 'that people are more willing to help the fallen than to help prevent the fall.'

46

It was the end of the day and the Rabbi sat by the bed of Lutnik the Draper who was also nearly at the end of his day. He and the Rabbi had been friends for a long time and Lutnik, though very sick, sensed the sadness in the Rabbi.

'Cheer up, Mark,' he said. 'We've had good times, you and I. Rich times – and sometimes not so rich times. Eh, my speculator?'

Mark was puzzled and then remembered how Lutnik had led him long ago into an investment with hard-earned savings. 'Can't fail,' Lutnik had said. 'Like planting kopeks to grow roubles. I'm putting in every penny of my own.' And he had. And the kopeks died in the ground and the roubles never grew and all was lost. The Rabbi lost only his savings but Lutnik lost everything. When Mark, upset and angry, had gone to the draper, he had found him at peace, behind his counter sorting socks.

'How can you be so calm, so – so – happy?' Mark had shouted.

Lutnik had put down the socks. 'God is good,' he said. 'He gave me a quick mind. The worrying and regret that would take other people a year I can finish in an hour.'

And Mark had learned a lesson and been grateful, and as the years passed had come to admire the old draper more and more. Lutnik was not a very observing Jew and indeed had not lived a very good life. He had a sharp tongue and could use it unsparingly on those he considered puffed-up or false. He made enemies and neglected his friends. He was an odd mixture of quick kindliness and an acid clear-eyed truthfulness too much for most people. He had not been too faithful to his wife but missed her sorely when she died. Now it was nearly his turn and he had no complaints. 'I'll be nicer to my Annie when we meet next time,' he said. 'That's if I go to the same place.'

The Rabbi listened and smiled reassuringly. Irascible and self-sufficient as the old man had always been, for the last year or two this thing of which place he was going to had come up more than once. First as a joke and then more seriously.

'I think you and Annie will meet in the same place,' said Mark.

'I think so too,' said Lutnik. 'And I want to thank you, Rabbi, for making it so easy.'

'Me?' said Mark.

'You,' said Lutnik, his eyes a little too bright

178

and his voice a little fainter. 'A while back I asked you what a man must do to get into Heaven and you said he should give to the poor, care for the sick and help the dead to decent burial.'

'I remember,' said Mark gently. 'Don't worry about it, old friend.'

'I did it,' chuckled Lutnik. Then he paused, for the chuckle had hurt him. 'I did it. I gave to a poor man who became sick so I took him into my house and looked after him but he got worse and died and I paid for his funeral. All in five weeks. And a ticket to see Annie. Why didn't you tell me it was so easy? Goodbye, Rabbi. Look after yourself.'

Mark waited till the end and when it was over felt lonely. Another lesson from Lutnik.

47

The Rabbi walked home by the little river. It was the longer way but prettier and for one day he'd had enough of people and wanted to walk slowly and not meet anyone. Just to see trees and flowers and have the sounds of the water for company. Sophie was right; 'Our town,' she would say, 'contains all the lunacies of a big city, so why move?' And they had stayed and the Rabbi had grown middle-aged and much respected for his fair judgment in the many disputes brought to him. 'Mark, how can you bear it?' Sophie would ask. 'Day after day. It would drive me out of my mind. How? Tell me.'

He would grin and say, 'With the two things I was born with. Patience and a sense of humour.'

Only that morning the case of Grand Larceny. The woman who'd accused her servant girl of stealing three pounds of meat. The defence: that the cat had stolen and eaten it. Mark believed the girl.

'Bring the cat,' he ordered. 'And weigh it!'

'But it happened yesterday,' said the girl.

'No matter!' said Mark the Great Judge. 'What does the cat weigh?'

'Three pounds,' said the cat-weigher.

'There is your meat!' roared Mark in a great voice, and the woman went away satisfied. 'But where,' said Mark to the servant, 'is the cat?'

When Mark reached home Sophie was waiting. She'd heard about the cat. 'This is better than the cat,' she said. 'In the parlour. A dispute on the naming of a first-born son. Go, great judge in Israel. You can have your supper afterwards.'

Mark knew the couple. He'd married them. They both looked flushed and angry and started to talk together, at once. He told them to wait while he put on his slippers, and took his time. No sign of the baby. 'Mother has him,' said the young wife. 'Your mother,' said her husband. 'Don't you begin on my mother,' said the wife. 'Your mother,' said the husband.

'Let us,' said Mark, 'stay with the problem. The child's name.'

'He will be named after my father,' said the young woman. 'Not his; mine.'

'NO!' yelled her husband. 'Not yours! MINE!'

Mark held up a hand and the fighting stopped. He had a slightly dizzy feeling. 'I know both your families well,' he said. 'And unless I am mistaken your two fathers have the same name. Samuel. Am I right?'

'Correct,' said the husband.

'Quite right,' said his wife.

'Proceed,' said Mark.

'The baby,' said the wife, 'will be named Samuel. After *my* father, who is a scholar and a gentleman and an orthodox Jew. Not after *his* father, who is a gambler and a drinker and never goes near a synagogue!'

The shouting began again and Mark could see Sophie looking at him through the nearly-closed door, her handkerchief stuffed in her mouth, her eyes dancing.

Mark put on his judge face. 'Name the child Samuel,' he said in a loud clear voice and the shouting stopped. 'And have patience and trust in God who will help you to bring him up. There will come a time when you will know exactly whose father he is named after. Live in peace. Love one another.'

Sophie saw them out and came back. 'I love you,' she said.

'Which shows you also are a good judge,' said Mark.

48

In the little town of Klaneshtetl no shops were open. The streets were clear. All was quiet. It was the Day of Atonement and the little synagogue was packed to the doors, as always on that Day when a man fasts from sundown to sundown and reviews his transgressions and asks forgiveness of his Maker.

It was the late afternoon. The Rabbi was feeling a bit tired and headachey. He could see by the angle of the beam of sunlight across the back wall that there was about another two hours to go till the end of the Fast. He had been in the synagogue since the start, the evening before, a lot of the time on his feet. Not everyone had stayed all night. Most had gone home to their beds, but in a way Mark preferred the night of that special Day. The very devout old men stayed, sometimes with a loving son or son-in-law. A Rabbinical student or two. Sometimes an equally devout woman, upstairs, in the gallery. And always, some of the ordinary townspeople, who felt a special atmosphere in the night hours, as he did.

Now the synagogue was full again, and the noise of prayer and singing was at its height. Sonorous, warm, with often the sound of tears from the women up above.

Mark looked around. How well he knew the town. Twenty-five years he'd been their Rabbi and he knew everybody. The very poor, the not so poor. The defeated and the successful. The good and the bad. The honest and the rascally. They could be maddening, his flock, with their narrow small-town minds and their dislikes and prejudices and superstititons. And yet, thought Mark, and yet, every now and then. . . .

His gaze fell upon a little man down to his left, quite near. The man was a cobbler. A widower, called Motel. A poor man, whose own boots badly needed the skills he had. He stood now in a large prayer shawl swaying with the others, his eyes closed, lips moving, book in hand. Book? thought Mark. Motel with a *book*? Motel can neither read nor write. A foot measure he can read, nothing else. Mark caught a word and bent a little to hear better amidst the drone of prayer.

'– and I've done what I should on this day, Almighty,' Motel was saying. 'I've listed my sins for forgiveness and atonement. The things I should repent. To be honest, the list doesn't come to much. Some bad things I've wished people who won't pay me. Some working on the Sabbath when things were bad. Some unkosher food. Compared to what you get up to, Almighty, a nothing. You took my Rachel in childbirth, and the child also. You allow pogroms, wars, pestilence, disease, drought, flood, massacres, wickedness, everything. So listen, Almighty, I'll tell you! I'll forgive you and you forgive me.'

Motel opened his eyes and Mark looked away, but Motel knew he'd been heard. The service went on, the sun went down, the ram's horn rang out and the Fast was over. People wished each other well and went to their homes.

As Mark locked up the synagogue, he saw Motel waiting for him.

The cobbler came closer. 'Did I do wrong, Rabbi?' he asked.

'No,' said Mark. 'You were foolish. You let God off too easily. With that list you could have asked forgiveness for the whole town. Come, Motel, come and break your fast with us.'

49

The Rabbi was stuck for a sermon. It happened now and then. Sophie knew all the signs. There would be a lot of wandering about the house by her Mark, a lot of picking up and putting down of books, little visits to her in the kitchen for glasses of tea, with long silences between sips. Sophie also knew that to be a Rebbitzen meant more than being a Rabbi's wife.

During the third or fourth tea-visit she said firmly, 'There are people in this town who "observe", who "practice", who are regular attenders of services and know all the prayers, and who also overwork their employees or servants for wages that are too low or no wages at all. A disgrace. Somebody should say or do something.'

Mark knew it was true. Even in a small town like Klaneshtetl there was much exploitation. People were poor and put up with a lot, out of fear. Many sizeable enterprises and farms in the area had been built on underpaid labour – or labour of a live-in all-found kind in very poor conditions indeed.

'Go for a walk, Mark,' said Sophie. 'Have a think. After all, you are an underpaid servant yourself.'

Mark walked, and thought, and leaned on gates and thanked God, as often before, for his beloved Sophie.

Sabbath came and the morning service was normal and standard. Mark looked around before he began his sermon. There seemed a fair number of Sophie's 'observers' and 'practisers', he thought, or maybe Sophie had made him see more clearly than before. It wouldn't be the first time. Here and there some of the underpaid and not-paid too. Ah well, thought Mark, and began.

'Once upon a time, long ago or last year or next week . . .' It was a good opening and Mark knew it and made a most actorish pause, with a glance up at Sophie in the women's gallery. She winked. 'There was,' Mark went on, 'an upright strict man who lived in a fine house and ran a big business. Every Sabbath he worshipped and on all the High Days and Holy Days. He fasted and he feasted. He had friends like himself and they were as self-satisfied as he was. He had an old servant called Pertchik who did far too much for the tiny wage he was paid. Pertchik's wife became ill, needing medicines and good food to eat. Pertchik knew that there would be neither help nor interest from his employer, so he started to steal from him. A few coins, some food, an extra blanket for his wife. God observed this and sent the Spirit of Goodness to see Pertchik, who was astonished but explained to Goodness that such stealing was essential. Goodness, who knew that Pertchik was a simple good man but rather timid, asked how he could help.

' "Perhaps," said Pertchik to Goodness, "if you went to my master and explained, he might help in some way. A little more money, a house not quite so damp."

' "I would with pleasure," said Goodness, "but he does not know of me. I've been to his door a number of times but have never been allowed to enter. I'm a stranger to him. I have never been in his home. You see, Pertchik," said Goodness sadly, "some people, even thieves like you, know me right away. To others, even strictly-observing and regularly-worshipping others, I am invisible and without influence of any kind. They seem to do better without Goodness." '

Mark had little hope that the point would be taken, but he felt better for trying

The Diary of Anne Frank 75p

The intimate record of a young girl's thoughts written during two years in hiding from the Gestapo, to whom she was at last betrayed.

The *Diary* has appeared in twenty-eight languages, and over a million copies have been sold in Pan alone.

'Few more moving and impressive books have come out of the war'
NAOMI LEWIS, OBSERVER

Ernst Schnabel
The Footsteps of Anne Frank 75p

The diary of Anne Frank ended abruptly on 1 August 1944. Three days later the Gestapo arrived, seized Anne and her family from their Amsterdam attic – and started them on their journey to Auschwitz and to Belsen.

The millions who have read *The Diary of Anne Frank* knew about Anne only what she herself disclosed in its pages; but Schnabel's book – a poignant epilogue to the amazing *Diary* gives us Anne's full story. Through the testimony of her father and friends, Ernst Schnabel has redrawn her happy childhood, her life in hiding, the family's betrayal and its disastrous aftermath – which only the father survived.

Slavomir Rawicz
The Long Walk 70p

The stirring account of one of the most terrible journeys ever made by man.

In a desperate bid to escape the inhuman cruelties of the Soviet Secret Police, Polish officer Slavomir Rawicz and six companions escaped from a prison camp in the Arctic Circle and in a year walked 4,000 miles to India.

Lauren Elder with Shirley Streshinsky
And I Alone Survived 90p

Not since *Alive!* has there been a survival story like this one.

Lauren Elder set out in a light aircraft with the pilot and his girlfriend on a joyride, skyborne sightseeing over the splendour of the Sierra Nevada range. When the plane hit the mountain, the joyride turned into a nightmare. After a night of sub-zero temperatures, Lauren, the only survivor, faced a fearsome 8000-feet climb down to safety . . .

'Vividly recreates a nightmare ordeal' YORKSHIRE POST

Farley Mowat
The Serpent's Coil 70p

The great sea saga of ships and men and the savage fury of a North Atlantic hurricane . . . the crushing embrace of the 'serpent's coil'.

'The true story of the Liberty ship *Leicester* which sailed for New York from England in the summer of 1948, ran into a hurricane and was abandoned with the loss of six lives in mid-Atlantic . . . and of the tug *Foundation Josephine* which tracked the derelict over many thousands of miles' NEW YORKER

The Grey Seas Under 75p

The North Atlantic is a hungry ocean . . . Across the wild seascape of gale and ice, hurricane and shrouds of ever-present fog, worked the tug *Foundation Franklin* and her colourful crew of Newfoundlanders. The story of how for fifteen years the *Franklin* rescued the great ships buffeted by wind, storm and sea, in peace and war, is unforgettable adventure reading.

'He writes with the authority of a sailor in his element'
NICHOLAS MONSARRAT

Bestselling Fiction and Non-Fiction

☐ Modesty Blaise	Peter O'Donnell	95p
☐ Falconhurst Fancy	Kyle Onstott	£1.50p
☐ The Pan Book of Card Games	Hubert Phillips	£1.25p
☐ The New Small Garden	C. E. Lucas Phillips	£2.50p
☐ Fools Die	Mario Puzo	£1.50p
☐ Everything Your Doctor Would Tell You If He Had the Time	Claire Rayner	£4.95p
☐ Polonaise	Piers Paul Read	95p
☐ The 65th Tape	Frank Ross	£1.25p
☐ Nightwork	Irwin Shaw	£1.25p
☐ Bloodline	Sidney Sheldon	95p
☐ A Town Like Alice	Nevil Shute	£1.25p
☐ Lifeboat VC	Ian Skidmore	£1.00p
☐ Just Off the Motorway	John Slater	£1.95p
☐ Wild Justice	Wilbur Smith	£1.50p
☐ The Spoiled Earth	Jessica Stirling	£1.75p
☐ That Old Gang of Mine	Leslie Thomas	£1.25p
☐ Caldo Largo	Earl Thompson	£1.50p
☐ Future Shock	Alvin Toffler	£1.95p
☐ The Visual Dictionary of Sex	Eric J. Trimmer	£5.95p
☐ The Flier's Handbook		£4.95p

All these books are available at your local bookshop or newsagent, or can be ordered direct from the publisher. Indicate the number of copies required and fill in the form below

Name _____
(block letters please)

Address _____

Send to Pan Books (CS Department), Cavaye Place, London SW10 9PG
Please enclose remittance to the value of the cover price plus:

25p for the first book plus 10p per copy for each additional book ordered to a maximum charge of £1.05 to cover postage and packing
Applicable only in the UK

While every effort is made to keep prices low, it is sometimes necessary to increase prices at short notice. Pan Books reserve the right to show on covers and charge new retail prices which may differ from those advertised in the text or elsewhere